Cover illustration by:

Elizabeth Carroll

Sound the Warning

Children of the World, Book 1

By Christie A. Sever

CHAPTER 1

When Thursday's school bell rang at 3 p.m., Joe and Isabel Scout had no idea that their vicious fight would ultimately lead them to a medieval castle. As they joined the rest of the kids bolting out of the school that sunny afternoon, they thought it was just an ordinary day in an ordinary week in a leafy green suburb of Chicago.

Joe caught up with his best friends. "Watch this," he laughed as he picked up a fallen tree limb. He sneaked up behind his twin sister, Isabel, as she chatted with her girlfriends. Joe slid the end of the stick through the straps on Isabel's backpack. Then he whipped the backpack away from her and ran off down the sidewalk.

"Joe Scout, come back here!" Izzy screamed chasing after him.

"Screecher Creature!" Joe shouted at her. He just loved calling her that name because it made her so mad. Sometimes it made her yell even more.

Izzy caught sight of her Mom in the minivan waiting in the pickup lane. "Mom! Joe stole my backpack!"

Mrs. Scout got out of the car and froze Joe with one of her silent You'd Better Watch It Young Man stares. "Joe, get in the car. And for heaven's sake put that dangerous stick down. You could hurt someone waving that thing around like that."

A few seconds later the other three neighborhood kids in the carpool joined them and they all piled into the minivan. Izzy plunked herself down in the front seat. She turned around to face the other kids and holding up a pretend microphone to her mouth announced, "Be sure to put your seatbelts on, contestants. Mom won't start the car until everyone's buckled up. And your time begins …… now!"

Joe grunted. "You're so bossy. And you're so freakishly addicted to TV game shows. Why can't I have a sister who's cool instead of this Screecher Creature."

Mrs. Scout pulled away from the curb. "F.L., Joe."

"What's F.L. mean, Joe?" asked one of the other boys.

Joe rolled his eyes. "It stands for Family Loyalty. My parents are always after us to stick up for each other, but they don't know how hard it is when you have a sister like Izzy. So, like this weekend, I really want to go hang out with my friend, Tom, but instead I have to blow a whole day watching my sister dance in an Irish dance competition. Do you believe that?" Joe slumped down in his seat. One of the other kids shook his head in sympathy. He had a bossy sister too.

Izzy turned around to face him. "Well, it's not so easy showing family loyalty to you either, Joe. How many of your soccer games have I suffered through? And your teasing and name-calling is SO annoying and juvenile."

"Well, if you weren't so bossy and loud and talkative and just so ...so...Izzy-like, maybe I wouldn't tease you," he replied.

"If I'm talkative, it's because I have so many interesting things to say. Unlike you! And now it's time for 'Family Feud'!"

"Enough!" Mrs. Scout barked at them both. "Your bickering is aggravating me to no end. You'd think that twins would be a lot closer and more loving to each other." She pulled into the neighbors' drives and let the other kids out. "Now, as soon as we get home, Joe, start on your homework, and Izzy you have to get ready to go to your last dance practice before the competition. And NO MORE FIGHTING!"

Later that afternoon, as soon as Izzy stepped into the dance studio she had a feeling she was going to have a good practice. Her fight with Joe earlier in the day lit her up with a certain tense fire and she had a lot of angry feelings to work out. Dancing vigorously always helped her vent her feelings.

After all the dancers had warmed up, their instructor, Natalie, called them all over for a meeting. "All right," she said. "Today we're going to do something special because it's the last practice before the competition. I want to have you all compete against each other to get ready for the weekend. You're each going to run through your solo set dances and the best competitor will get a prize from my prize box. Now, who wants to go first?"

Izzy loved her set dance. Each Irish set dance was given a name and the steps were identical whether they were performed in Chicago, Illinois; Sydney, Australia or Dublin, Ireland. Her set dance's name was "Sound the Warning." She wore her hard shoes that made a loud racket as she stamped out the steps on the wooden floor. When she practiced at home, Joe would run screaming from the practice room because she was so loud. Maybe that was another reason why she liked her set dance.

She was the third person in the class to compete. As she waited for the musical introduction before beginning, she checked out her image in the wall mirror. Her long hair was clutched into a ponytail, she wore a tee shirt and practice shorts, and her white poodle socks rose above her hard shoes. Her fists were clenched straight down at her side, and she held her head up high with perfect posture. Then at her musical cue, she flew into the "Sound the Warning" set dance. Her stamps were loud and strong, her leaps were high and her turns were crisp. Every step fused perfectly with the music. When she finished, sweat was dripping off her face and running down her back. As she stood, chest heaving from exertion, waiting for Natalie's comments, she knew she had danced well. She imagined herself as one of the contestants on 'Dancing with the Stars' facing the three judges. Natalie smiled at her and said, "Well done, Izzy. That was beautifully performed. Just watch your foot placement at the end."

After all the kids had danced their sets, Natalie looked over the class. "Most of you danced really well. I can tell you've been practicing. I think you'll perform particularly well this weekend at the competition. The winner of the prize this afternoon is.......Isabel Scout! Come on up, Izzy, and pick something from the prize box."

Thrilled to be selected, Izzy skipped over to the prize box, closed her eyes, and reached into the box. Her hand closed upon something hard about the size of a skipping stone that she and Joe would skim on the surface of the lake. She pulled

it out. It looked like some kind of old jewelry.
There was a round glittery crystal surrounded by
some curlicue metal decoration. There was a pin
on the back. She looked up at Natalie and asked,
"What is it?"

Natalie smiled at her. "That is an antique
brooch that belonged a long time ago to someone
in my family. I think it was probably used to pin
an old-timey shawl together. I have a bunch of
them and can't really use this one myself. It might
look really pretty if you shine it up properly."

"Thanks, Natalie, I will," Izzy said and she
dropped her prize in her dance bag.

That night after dinner, she found some
polish and a rag and rubbed hard on the crystal
and the metal holding it. Natalie was right. After
a little hard work, the crystal glistened and the
metal gleamed. She peered closer at the brooch.
The metal had been formed into the shapes of a
crown, a heart and some hands. It was really
quite pretty; although not something she would
ever consider wearing because it was so old-
fashioned looking. She dropped it into her jacket

pocket to bring to school tomorrow to show her friends.

CHAPTER 2

Friday morning began normally enough as both Joe and Isabel waited for the best part of the day – recess. It was a beautiful sunny spring day and all the kids were happy to get out of the stuffy school building and run around the playground at noon.

Joe met up with his buddies and started kicking the soccer ball around. It wouldn't be long before they were all huffing and puffing over the game. Most of them played together on the park district team and they all loved any extra practice time they could get. Soon Joe's dark hair was matted down around his face and there were dark circles of sweat under the sleeves of his shirt.

Izzy found her girlfriends and began at once to talk about the prize she had won at her Irish dance class the night before. "Well let's see this weird and wonderful brooch thing then," her best friend Carolyn encouraged.

Izzy dug into her jacket pocket and felt around. She frowned. "It's not here. I put it here last night so I could show you..." She started emptying her pocket. There were some tissues, some Jolly Ranchers and a hair clip. But there was no brooch. "Oh no!" she moaned as her fingers reached the bottom of her pocket and discovered a large hole in the corner of the pocket. "It must have fallen out of my pocket. I've been depocketed. Wait, is that even a word? Anyway, let's try to find it." The girls spread apart and began to scour the ground looking for Izzy's prize.

Meanwhile, on the other side of the playground, Joe booted a perfect line drive into the soccer net. He fist-pumped the air and high-fived his cheering teammates. Then he jogged over to the sideline to catch his breath. As he sat down on the ground, something sharp and hurtful poked into his rear end. He scooched over to see what it was. "Wow, look at this!" he shouted to his friends as he picked up a very old-looking sparkly piece of jewelry. His friends crowded around him. "What the heck is that?" someone said. "I don't know, but I bet it's worth about a million dollars," someone else offered.

They were causing such an excited commotion that a lot of other kids ran over to see what was happening. Izzy and her friends joined the group. When Izzy saw what Joe was holding, she let out a happy shout. "Joe! You found my brooch! We've been looking all over for it." She moved to snatch it out of Joe's hand.

He quickly closed his fingers over the brooch and pulled his hand away from her. "YOUR brooch? What are you talking about? I just found it right now. I was sitting on it. You weren't even near it." The other soccer boys nodded.

"It IS mine. I won it last night at dance practice. I brought it to school today. It must have fallen out of my pocket. Now give it back to me." She lunged for his hand.

Joe didn't know if it belonged to her or not but he really didn't like her tone. "There she goes, being bossy again," he thought. "She's trying to make me look bad in front of my friends. I'll show her." He took off running away from her. "Try to catch me!" he yelled at her. Izzy screamed at him and tried to catch up but he really was a very fast runner. Before long the entire playground was shouting and egging on either Joe or Izzy. The twins were hurling insults and names at each other and definitely not showing any family loyalty.

The playground commotion brought Ms. Lyons to the scene. She was the most ferocious teacher of them all. She quickly cornered Joe as he was looking backwards and taunting Izzy, and grabbed the collar of his jacket. Izzy caught up to the two of them. Ms. Lyons grabbed Izzy's collar as well and marched the two of them back into the school and right into Principal Grady's office.

"Mr. G.," she said, plunking the two of them down in the chairs in front of his desk. These two were fighting like cats and dogs at recess and disturbing the entire playground. "Thank you, Ms. Lyons," said Mr. G. "I'll take it from here."

As Ms. Lyons left, Mr. G. looked from one of them to the other. He sighed and rubbed his hands over his face. Joe and Izzy sat quietly, wondering what was going to happen to them, and how they were going to explain to their mom that they had been brought to the Principal's office yet again.

"Isabel, what is this all about?" he asked.

"Well, I won a brooch at dance class last night, and I lost it on the playground. Joe found it but he won't give it back to me," she said.

"Joe? What's your side of the story?"

"It isn't her brooch, whatever that is, at all," Joe started, glaring hard at Izzy. "I found it fair and square. She saw me getting all sorts of attention and decided that she wanted to take it. She tried to steal it from me."

"But it's mine!" Izzy cried.

"Nope, you can't prove that," said Joe.

Mr. G. stood up and held out his hand. "Ok, because neither one of you can prove that it is yours, you will give it to me." Joe grudgingly handed Mr. G. the brooch. He continued, "The two of you really need to get along better. You're twins after all. You share so much family history. Someday, I hope you will be best of friends. But until then, you both need to cool down and serve a little time in detention. Come with me." As they left his office, he let them stop at their lockers and pick up their backpacks.

Mr. G. led the twins down the hallway to the detention room. It was a little used classroom at the end of the hall filled with some desks, old science projects, music stands and outdated maps. The only other person in the room was Old Mrs. Sanow. She was nodding off at the teacher's desk.

"Mrs. Sanow," said Mr. G, "the Scout twins will spend the rest of recess in detention today. They have been fighting over this little piece of jewelry. I'm going to put it here," and he placed it on the window sill. "They will both use their detention time to write a short essay on their tablets. The topic of the essay will be 'Why It's Important to Get Along With my Family'. Will you please keep an eye on them and release them when the afternoon class bell sounds?"

"Yes sir," said Mrs. Sanow, scowling at the twins. "I'll make sure they behave."

"Thank you," said Mr. G. and he left the room, closing the door behind him.

CHAPTER 3

Mrs. Sanow stood up and folded her arms in front of her. She might be old, but she could still be mean. "Well, take your seats," Mrs. Sanow said. "You heard what the principal said. You'd better get busy on those essays." She rambled back to her desk, opened a book and got comfy again.

"Ugh," Joe thought. "What a waste of a perfectly good recess." But he pulled out his tablet from his backpack and started tapping away.

Izzy slumped down in her desk furious at the way the afternoon was shaping up. It just wasn't fair. Not only did she lose her brooch, but Joe found it and wouldn't give it back. Then they got into another fight and now she was stuck in detention. It wasn't fair at all. She felt the edges of her eyes start to sting and her lips were tugging downward. "Oh no," she thought. "Now I'm going to start to cry and Joe is just going to laugh at me and tease me even more."

Izzy glanced over at Mrs. Sanow who was starting to nod off again. Izzy thought, "Easy for her to nap, life isn't unfair for her." Then she looked over to the window sill where Mr. G. had placed the brooch.

The sunlight from the window was hitting the sparkly part of the brooch and making a rainbow beam squirt out of the opposite end. The rainbow beam was the most beautiful thing she had ever seen. Every color was there – red, orange, yellow, green, blue and vivid violet. It was just like the perfect rainbows formed by prisms she had studied in science class. She followed the beam with her eyes to see where it ended. The rainbow beam ended on the classroom wall where an old dusty pull-down map of the world hung. Bits of dust were suspended in the beam and glittered as they twirled about in the air. It was almost hypnotizing to watch.

Izzy looked over at Mrs. Sanow who by now was sound asleep at her desk again. Izzy slowly rose from her desk and moved quietly over to the rainbow beam. She squinched up her eyes to see where the beam hit the map.

"What are you doing?" asked Joe, looking up from his essay.

"Shhh!" Izzy put her finger to her lips. "Come here and look at this."

Joe stuffed his tablet in his backpack, slung it over his shoulder, and crept past Mrs. Sanow to where Izzy stood in front of the map. He saw the rainbow from the brooch ending on the map. At its end, it was swirling just a little bit on an island in the Atlantic Ocean.

"That's cool!" he said, peering closer at the map. "It looks like it's just disappearing into that island."

"Quiet!" hissed Izzy. "You'll wake Mrs. Sanow."

Joe glanced back at the teacher. "Nope, she's asleep. I think she was born in the 18th century, she's so old." Just as he was saying that, he touched his finger to the island on the map where the rainbow ended.

Joe's eyes widened as a shock of electricity jolted through his finger. His other hand shot out and grabbed Izzy. She felt the electric current tingle through her whole body. Then, incredibly, it felt like the two of them were being sucked into the map. They didn't have any time to think. Before they knew it they were hurtling through a space filled with all the colors of the rainbow beam. It felt as though they were flying faster than an airplane, or maybe even a rocket. Izzy's long hair was whipping back and forth across her face. She grabbed tighter onto Joe's hand as the wind rushed past her. Joe's face looked all pulled back like it did when they were flying down the biggest drop on the roller coaster. His mouth was wide open but no sound was coming out of it. No one could hear anything anyway because of the booming rushing noise that was filling the air. They felt like they were caught up in a tornado or a hurricane. They couldn't see the ground and there wasn't any sky. Just crazy kaleidoscope rainbow colors flying past them and the roaring blowing noise all around them.

Then, as suddenly as it started, it stopped.

The noisy rushing wind and the pulling forces suddenly let go of them and they plopped down to the ground, thudding onto a soft green mat of grass. A puff of shamrocks settled softly around them. Izzy's hair whispered back down around her shoulders. Joe and Izzy stared wide-eyed at each other.

"THAT," declared Joe "was EPIC!"

CHAPTER 4

They looked around them. They were sitting in the greenest world they had ever seen. They were surrounded by lush green grass spreading out to distant green clumps of trees. Everywhere the color was such an intense emerald green…not like the grass and trees at home that sometimes had little smudges of yellow or brown in them. This was the vibrant green of a sunlit lily pad. The sky above was blue with puffy white clouds scudding across. The air felt soft and moist, somehow, like all the harshness of the world had been worn out of it.

"But where are we?" asked Izzy. "Where are Mrs. Sanow and our school? Where are Burr Oaks Glen and our parents and our friends?" She looked so confused. "I mean, what just happened?" She stood up and turned around looking in every direction. Nothing looked familiar.

Joe stood up and looked around. There were green hills rolling all the way to the horizon.

Riding along the green hills were long stone fences that came up to his waist. They were made out of stones that had been piled on top of each other. He saw little clumps of trees and fields that looked as though they were being farmed. Off in the distance was a collection of white sheep with plump behinds. His soccer instinct immediately kicked in and he felt like he wanted to punt the sheep one by one over those stone fences. He didn't see any buildings.

"Wow," said Joe. "I have no clue where we are. This sure doesn't look like Burr Oaks Glen." He frowned in thought. "Hey! I have an idea. My tablet is in my backpack. Let's just check the GPS and find out where we are."

"Oh good," said Izzy and she moved near him and looked over his shoulder. He reached into his backpack, pulled out the I Pad and fired it up. They waited a few seconds.

"Hmmm," frowned Joe. "It looks like the network is down or something. I can't get the internet to work at all."

"Is the battery low?" asked Izzy, looking over his shoulder.

"No, Joe answered, tapping some keys, "all the other apps are working just fine. I just can't get internet service. That's weird. I wonder what's ....."

He wasn't able to finish his sentence, because just then something from behind him slammed him down to the ground. "Hey!" he shouted but his face was pushed into the grass. He heard Izzy scream as she was forced to the ground as well. He felt strong arms, many of them, grappling with his own arms, pinning them. Someone was sitting on top of him and he couldn't move at all.

"Get his gold!" someone behind him shouted.

Izzy had been pushed to the ground as well and she could see two girls who were holding her arms down. She looked over at Joe and saw two boys sitting on top of his back and a third boy circling around him tugging at his backpack. She felt like they were being mugged. She needed to call for the police and she let loose with one of her very loudest Screecher Creature screams. The five robbing children stopped what they were doing and stared at her.

"It's a Banshee!!!!!" they yelped. They almost ran away. But one of the older muggers shook his head. "She might very well be a Banshee, but she can't hurt us here. Let's just get the gold and be off."

"You," the older boy glared at Izzy, "No more of your shenanigans. Be quiet or you'll be sorry!"

"Now, where's your gold, you squirmy leprechaun?" One of the smaller boys pulled Joe's backpack out from under him and began rooting through the contents. He wasn't finding what he was looking for so he turned the backpack upside down and shook out all the contents. The other two boys who were holding Joe down looked over at the smaller boy. "Check those pockets with the strange metal tracks." The smaller boy tugged at the zipper pulls and reached around in the pockets, scattering all the contents on the ground. They examined the objects on the ground. There were books, a pencil case, a water bottle, Joe's lunch, some folders, and a hackeysack. There was no gold.

"All right, you crafty leprechaun, where is it?" they demanded of Joe. "Where's your gold? And don't you be lying to us now. We caught you fair and square."

Joe tried to answer the boy, but his mouth was smushed into the grass and all that came out was a muffled, "mmph mmph."

The smaller boy waved at Joe, and said, "All right, lads, let him sit up. But keep your arms on his hands and legs so he doesn't scurry off on us."

Joe sat up, with the two bigger boys pinning down his arms and legs. He looked over to where Izzy was still being held down by the two girls. There were bits of grass stuck in her hair and she looked totally bewildered. Then he took a longer look at the five children who had captured them. All five of them had pale skin with scatterings of freckles across their faces. The youngest girl was maybe 3 years old and the oldest boy looked like he was about 14. The two girls were dressed in long heavy skirts that came down to the ground. They wore shawls about their shoulders and bonnets covering their long hair. The boys seemed to be dressed in very old-fashioned pants and jackets. Their shoes looked more like hiking boots than the gym shoes that he and his friends all wore. Sheep wandered around them "baa-ing" softly and ripping up tufts of grass with their mouths. Joe felt like he was watching characters in a Disney movie.

Was he dreaming? No, he thought, someone's sharp elbow was poking him in the ribs. This was no dream.

CHAPTER 5

"Well?" demanded the smaller boy, shaking Joe's backpack at him, "Where are your riches, leprechaun?"

Joe frowned and shook his head. "All I have is in that backpack. I don't have any riches or gold. And why do you keep calling me a leprechaun?"

One of the older boys holding Joe spat away in contempt. "Oh get off your high horse; we know you're a leprechaun. How else do you explain the fact that you just magically appear in a poof in the middle of our field and scare all our sheep? You didn't just drop out of the sky. And you're dressed so crazy, we know you're trying to disguise yourself."

Joe turned to him. "I honestly don't know how we arrived here. We were just following this rainbow and ..."

"HA! Gotcha there, boyo!" said the older boy, giving the others a knowing look. "Everyone knows that leprechauns hide their gold at the end of a rainbow. Now for the last time...where is it?" He bent down towards Joe with a fight in his face.

"Seriously, I'm NOT a leprechaun. The only leprechaun I know is on the box of Lucky Charms," said Joe, still trying to understand how he had gotten into this mess.

"Well," Izzy piped in helpfully. "There's also the leprechaun mascot for the Fighting Irish of Notre Dame. We know about that one too."

One of the girls holding Izzy turned to her. "And exactly WHAT do you know about the Fighting Irish?" she demanded. She gave the phrase "Fighting Irish" sort of a proud feel to it. "Are you a spy, Banshee?" She gave Izzy's arm a little twist.

"Ouch!" squealed Izzy. "I love the Fighting Irish," she said. "They're my favorite team in the entire world."

"Hmff," said the girl, relaxing her hold on Izzy. "We'll see about that."

"Well, Michael, what should we do about these two?" the smaller boy asked the oldest.

Michael stood up, forcing Joe to stand as well. "We shouldn't let them go. We should bring them back home and let Da figure out how to get their gold. Patrick, you collect all the leprechaun's belongings and put them back in his sack. Let's get the sheep rounded up and get on back before Ma and Da think we've been taken by the soldiers."

With that, one of the captors pulled long leather straps out of his pocket and tied Izzy and Joe's hands together. They rounded up the scattered sheep and their strange little parade tramped through the green fields in silence.

Joe briefly thought about breaking away and escaping, but with his hands tied up he wasn't likely to get very far before they caught him again. And he couldn't just leave Izzy alone to deal with the strange muggers. Just looking at her scared little face made him feel sort of protective of her. He had never felt that way before about his sister. But she was the only familiar thing in this strange new world.

Izzy was trying to sort through the jumble of sights, sounds and feelings colliding in her brain. She felt like a prisoner but she didn't think these strange children wanted to hurt them. One of them, the oldest, she thought his name was Michael, talked about bringing them to Da and Ma. Maybe the children were all brothers and sisters and were bringing them home to their parents. Maybe their parents could sort it all out. Maybe Izzy could borrow their phone and call her Mom and she could come pick them up.

She still didn't quite understand how they had traveled to this place from the detention classroom in the first place. And she didn't understand why these kids thought Joe was a leprechaun. And she really didn't understand why they kept calling her a Banshee and a spy. She didn't even know what a Banshee was.

After about 15 minutes, they crested the top of a hill and saw a cluster of little cottages below them in a small valley. Smoke curled out of the chimneys and several people were behind some of the cottages working the soil with hoes.

The sun was beginning to cast long shadows on the village.

They walked through a dirt lane between the cottages and turned off the lane at the third cottage. It had white walls and a thatched roof. The cottage had an enclosed yard around it with a low fence encircling it. The fence was made of small boulders piled on top of each other. Patrick opened a gate and prodded the sheep into the front yard enclosure.

"All right, Leprechaun and Banshee," he said. "It's time to meet your fate. Into the house you go."

CHAPTER 6

He opened the front door. It was a curious looking door. It was in two parts, an upper door and a lower door. The upper door was already open and acted as a sort of window. Patrick opened the lower door and led them in. As the children entered the cottage, they saw a humble two room home with a dirt floor. A long wooden table with chairs took up one end of the room and a large fireplace was at the other end. A delicious stew-smell reminded them that they hadn't eaten since breakfast. Bending over a cauldron at the open fire was a woman. She looked up and smiled as they entered. "Ah, my babies! You're just in time for dinner. But wait … who are these two?" she said pointing at Izzy and Joe with her stirring spoon.

Michael answered for them. "We caught them in the meadow. They are a leprechaun and a Banshee, but we can't find their gold. They're quite magical. We thought Da would help us."

At that, a strong looking man appeared from the next room holding a smoking pipe in his hands. "What's all this hubble-bubble?" he asked. His eyes narrowed as he saw Joe and Izzy. "What kind of children are these?"

His children started talking all at once describing how the two Scouts just appeared and came at the end of a rainbow and wore strange clothing and refused to give up their gold and screeched like a Banshee. Maybe they were spies as well.

"I see," he said. He narrowed his eyes and looked them over. "Michael," he said, "untie their hands." Izzy and Joe rubbed their wrists where the leather thongs had pressed into their skin. Then to the Scout twins he said, "Sit down at the table, you two." Joe and Izzy sat down, still looking very scared. "Now, tell me who you are and how you came to be here."

Izzy spoke up saying, "My name is Isabel, but my friends call me Izzy. This is my brother Joe." She then related the whole story about the detention classroom, the brooch, the rainbow, the crazy journey and the final thump down in the meadow. "We really don't mean any harm to anyone. In fact, we'd really just like to get back home. We're so very lost. We have no idea where we are. Could we please just borrow your phone and call our Mom so she can come pick us up?"

"Our phone, hmmm?" Da said.

"Or better yet," continued Joe, "could we please use your internet to map our way home?"

"Our internet?" asked Da.

"Yes," said Joe. "I wasn't able to get any reception out in the field." He pulled out his tablet and showed Da. Da took the tablet in his hand and looked at the screen. The screensaver was displaying moving images of sword fighting dudes and heroes with light sabers. Da's eyebrows shot way up high.

He passed the tablet around to the rest of the family. They seemed absolutely amazed to look at it.

"What IS that?" asked Patrick with amazement. He couldn't take his eyes off the screensaver.

Da puffed on his pipe a while. "Well, you two don't seem to be a leprechaun and a Banshee to me," he said. "But you and your moving slate here do seem to be pretty magical. And many magical things happen here in Ireland."

"IRELAND!" said Joe and Izzy together. "Is that where we are?"

"Well of course, sillies. Are you daft? And you are now in the cottage of the Murphy family. But here's the question, where are your parents?"

"Um, they're back in Burr Oaks Glen. That's in Illinois. In the United States," said Izzy.

"That was some rainbow trip," added Joe shaking his head.

"So may we borrow your phone please and call our parents?" asked Izzy.

Da frowned. "Lassie, I don't know what this phone is that you're talking about. And I don't know what the internet is. Furthermore, I haven't heard of this Illinois village. You two seem very confused to me. Maybe you hit your heads on your trip. I have heard of people losing their memories when their heads get bumped. Why don't you stay here for dinner and we'll try to figure out how to get you back to your parents."

He took a closer look at Izzy. "Ma, this poor lass seems to have lost her dress. Here she sits only in her undies. Please get her a shift to wear."

Izzy looked down at her legs. "These aren't my undies. They're my leggings."

Ma shook her head furiously at Izzy. "Come here dear. We'll help you with your modesty." And she led Izzy into the back room, rooted around in a dresser drawer and pulled out a long brown dress, similar to the ones her daughters were wearing. "Here, this should fit you well," and she left Izzy to pull it over her head.

When Izzy reappeared in the great room, Joe had to stifle a laugh as he saw his sister wearing such an old-fashioned dress. Izzy shot him a Don't You Dare look and sat down at the table with the others.

"Well now, Ma, that stew smells delicious. Let's dig in," said Da. As Ma ladled out the stew to everyone at the table, Izzy asked one of the daughters next to her why they wore such old-fashioned clothing.

"Old-fashioned?" replied Siobhan, the 12-year-old. "Why everyone wears dresses like these."

"Well, no offense now, but they look like they're from the 17th century or something," replied Izzy.

"Oh please," responded Siobhan. "We wouldn't wear anything so dated. This is quite modern for today. After all, it's 1785, and we don't want to be behind the times."

Izzy and Joe dropped their spoons at the same time, splattering a little of the stew. They gaped at each other, then at the family and the cottage in which they sat. "1785," said Joe slowly, thinking how this could be. "Oh my gosh! No wonder there's no phone or internet. Or even electricity ... and, well, even Illinois hasn't become a state yet. But, how....?"

Izzy drummed her fingers on the wooden table. "Joe, I've got it!" she said. "Remember when we were looking at the crystal rainbow that landed on the map? Just before we, er, got sucked into it….You looked at Mrs. Sanow and said that she was born in the 18th century. Just at the moment you said that, we were pulled into the map and landed where the beam ended – here in Ireland. You must have somehow given the crystal the command to place us where the beam ended at the specific time that you mentioned – 18th century Ireland."

Joe nodded slowly. "It's the only explanation. WE'VE TIME TRAVELLED! We're sitting here in Ireland in 1785. This is so incredibly awesome. I can't even believe it!"

"I know, right?" said Izzy. "This is amazing! I can't wait to tell Carolyn."

"Tom is never going to believe it. I can't believe we're in Ireland!" said Joe. "This sure beats that trip to New Orleans he was bragging about."

"But Joe, wait," said Izzy. "Somehow we have to get back. How on earth are we ever going to time travel back to Burr Oaks Glen? Will we ever see our parents or our friends again? Oh my gosh, they aren't even born yet!" and her hands flew up to her face in astonishment.

The twins looked around the table at the Irish family who had accepted them into their home and fed them dinner. The family had stopped eating and they were looking from one to the other in total bewilderment.

"I told you they were magical," said Michael with satisfaction.

CHAPTER 7

Later that evening when the dishes had been cleared away the family sat down before the fire. Ma and the two girls, Siobhan and Claire, took up balls of yarn, and started knitting near the light of the fire. Da lit up his pipe and sat back in a rocking chair. His sons, Michael, Patrick and Luke, sat on the floor around him. Michael picked up a tin whistle and played some lively tunes softly. Joe had never seen a tin whistle before. It looked a little like a baby flute made of rolled metal, with six holes along the tube. Michael held it straight in front of him and used his fingers to cover the holes and make a lively melody.

The grownups talked. "Ma," said Da. "I think these children are very confused. Let's foster them here until we can find their parents and return them."

"That's the right thing to do, Da," said Ma. "And my heart does go out to them. They seem so lost and alone. But as you know, we need to be very careful not to attract any attention from the soldiers. They must be taught how to act and what to say so that they don't bring trouble to this house." Da nodded.

"Joe and Isabel Scout come here," said Da. "Ma and I want you to stay with us until you can be returned to your parents. But there are some rules you need to follow here in the Murphy household."

The twins sat on the floor by Da's feet. "Thanks so much for dinner and for letting us stay here," said Izzy. "We can help clean the dishes, help mind the sheep, whatever you need. What other rules do we need to know?"

Da began talking, but there was something different about the words he was using. He glanced across at Ma as he was talking and she appeared to be looking closely at the twins to see their reactions. The twins both tilted their heads a little bit trying to understand what Da was saying. The words made sense, but they seemed different to them. Then Da was asking Joe a question. He said, "Joe, do you understand what I am saying?" Joe nodded and repeated what Da had just said.

Da seemed satisfied with Joe's answer. "Well fine, then. Sorry, children, but that was a little test. I needed to know that you understood the Irish language. I needed to make sure that you weren't English spies."

"I'm not sure I understand," said Joe. Izzy shrugged her shoulders. She couldn't figure out how they could understand the foreign language either.

"Well, you know it's all about the Penal Laws," said Da.

Joe laughed out loud. He nudged Patrick next to him saying, "Ha! Your dad just said Penal!" Patrick stared back at Joe.

Da smacked his hand down hard on the armrest of the rocker, startling the twins. "There is nothing funny about the Penal Laws!" he shouted as his face bloomed bright red. "You won't dare make light of them in the Murphy household."

"Gosh, I'm terribly sorry," said Joe. "But, but I'm afraid I don't know what they are." He looked so innocent and sincere that Da sat back staring at him. "You really don't know what they are, do you?"

Joe shook his head. Izzy shook hers too. They felt as if they had flunked a test. They had so much to learn here.

Da puffed on his pipe a little bit, thinking. Clouds of fragrant smoke rose slowly above him. "Well," he said. "You two really are terribly befuddled. Maybe you did hit your heads or something. But I don't think you're spies, because you understood the Irish language when I was speaking it to you a few minutes ago."

"You see," he continued. "The Penal Laws forbid us Irish people from speaking our own language. We speak English when we are out in public, just in case the English soldiers or their spies are around to listen to us. But in the privacy of our own homes we continue to speak our native language – the Irish language. When I was speaking to you in Irish a little while ago, you understood what I was saying, and you spoke it back to me, so I know that you're on our side."

"But why can't you speak your own Irish language if you're in Ireland?" asked Izzy.

"Ah, you see now," said Da. "That's because of the Penal Laws. It is a punishment to our land. The laws forbid us to speak our Irish language, play our Irish music, dance our Irish dance, go to Irish schools, or go to Irish churches. The British are attempting to kill our Irish culture entirely." Joe and Izzy's mouths dropped open in disbelief. These Penal Laws were ridiculously harsh. "But, of course, we rebel against this," continued Da. "We make sure to speak Irish when we are at home, and we play our music at home." He gazed fondly at Michael playing the tin whistle. "And when we can safely do so, we go to church, school and dance to keep our culture alive. They cannot crush our spirit or our culture."

"Well, I'm not quite sure how we understood the Irish language when Da was speaking it to us," muttered Izzy to Joe. "It must have something to do again with the magic crystal that got us here in the first place."

Joe lifted his eyebrows and shrugged. "Ireland is a magical place," he replied.

"Why are there Penal Laws anyway?" Izzy asked Da. "Did Ireland do something bad and needed to be punished?"

"No, lassie, Ireland didn't do anything bad," replied Da. "It all has to do with politics. There was a war about a hundred years ago. The people of Ireland supported King James, who was a Catholic in his war against William of Orange, who was the head of the Anglican church in England.

"Oh, wait! I know about that," said Izzy. "It was a question on 'Jeopardy'. Each of them wanted to rule England, right?"

"Yes, Izzy," said Da. "And the Irish were resisting increased British rule of our island. King James lost the war and the English wanted to make sure that such resistance never happened again. There have been restrictions on the freedoms of Irish people for a very long time. But once King James lost, the English created even more burdensome Penal Laws that attempt to crush any Irish identity and any Irish thoughts of independence from England. Anything Catholic is forbidden. No Catholic can vote or be elected to office. Catholics cannot own land. We cannot own weapons or even own a horse worth more than a pittance. We are required to pay money to the Anglican Church, which is not our church. "

"Wow," said Joe. "That seems really unfair."

"Well, of course it's unfair. And these Penal Laws are making Ireland poor. And that is why we rebel. But we cannot be too obvious about it, because there are English soldiers living here throughout Ireland ready to throw us into prison if we disobey their laws. And there are spies who are only too happy to turn us in for a cash reward. That is why we have to be so careful about letting in strangers like you."

Izzy was thinking about all Da had to say. She asked, "You said you cannot own land. But we are here in your cottage on some nice land with sheep in the pen."

Da turned to the side and spat into the fire. "You would think so, now, wouldn't you? But we don't own this land. And we don't own this cottage or the sheep. We rent it all from the English landlord. We farm his land and we tend his sheep. And we need to turn in almost all the money that we make from the sheep and the land."

"All of it?" asked Joe. "But how do you buy food and clothing?"

"We are given a small plot of land for ourselves. It is so small that all we can really grow on it are potatoes. All the farmers in this village grow potatoes for themselves. The rest of the food we have to scrounge to get. The Penal Laws are making Ireland poor."

Izzy turned to Ma. "But the stew was so good. It had more than potatoes in it."

Ma smiled. "Yes, it did. We are a lucky family. We live near the ocean so that the boys can fish. They are also good hunters, so we have small game to eat as well. We do the best we can, but it isn't easy. It would be a terrible thing if something happened to the potato crop, though. We depend on that vegetable tremendously.

Sometimes I wonder how our lovely country will get by if the potatoes ever fail."

"Hey," said Joe, turning to Patrick. "Your dad said that the laws forbid school. Does that mean that we don't have to go to school here?" Joe was clearly excited about the fact that he could fish and hunt all day and not have to worry about math, science or history tests while he was in Ireland.

"Not so fast," said Patrick sympathetically. "We do go to school. But it's called hedge school. And, yes, we have to go tomorrow. I guess you'll have to go with us."

"Hedge school? What's that?" asked Joe. "Is it a school outside near a hedge?"

"Well, sometimes they are outdoors, but mostly they're inside a barn," answered Patrick. "We Irish aren't allowed to have our own schools, so they're kind of a way to get around the law. They're secret, you see. Sometimes they're held in caves or little shepherds' huts or yes, behind bushes and hedges."

"Wow, secret! That's awesome!" said Joe.

"The teacher is very smart, but very strict too. His job is extremely dangerous."

"Dangerous?" asked Izzy. "Why?"

Luke added, "He could be arrested by the soldiers for disobeying the law ... by teaching us. So we lads all take turns keeping watch from the hilltop for the soldiers. Tomorrow, it's my turn," he said proudly.

Da stood up. "Before they're allowed outside, we have to teach young Joe and Isabel here how to conduct themselves if they run into any soldiers." He looked at his family. "Siobhan, you talk to them before we turn in for the night and let them know how to act and what to say."

Siobhan nodded. "Yes, Da."

Luke had an idea. "Say, why don't we bring them to Blarney after school tomorrow so that they will be able to speak better with the soldiers if they do get caught? Could I bring them there tomorrow, Da?"

Da smiled. "Yes, Luke. That's not a bad idea at all. We will make sure that they kiss the

Blarney stone so that they have the gift of gab as well. Now Siobhan, talk to the children and then, all of you off to bed."

After their quick lesson with Siobhan, the twins looked forward to bed. What an exhausting day! Izzy had wondered where they were going to sleep. It was only a two room cottage after all. Da draped his arm around Ma and the two of them disappeared into the back room. The five Murphy children and the two Scouts were to sleep all in the same room with the fireplace. The children unrolled pallets and blankets. Izzy and Joe were used to sleeping in their own rooms at home, so this was going to seem like a sleepover party to them. They were so tired that they probably could have slept standing up, but they gratefully accepted a pallet and blankets and curled up on the floor with the rest of the kids.

"Good night, Joe," said Izzy. All she received in response from her brother was a snore.

CHAPTER 8

"Seriously?" thought Joe as the first touch of dawn glanced through the window. "Am I really hearing a rooster?"

Sure enough a rooster was crowing outside. As Joe sat up rubbing his eyes he could hear Ma bustling around the room cooking up breakfast for the family. The other kids were moving about. Some were washing their faces and hands using a pitcher of water and a bowl at a small table near the door.

"Excuse me," said Joe. "Could you tell me where the bathroom is?"

Ma turned to Luke who was rolling up his pallet. "Luke, darling," she said, "Take young Joe here to the outhouse."

Joe's eyes bugged out. "Yikes!" he thought. "I have to use a stinky outhouse!"

Luke and Joe pulled on their shoes and went outside. Luke pointed to the outhouse at the edge of the lot. "There it is," he said. "Leave it clean."

Joe was pleasantly surprised that the outhouse was very clean, but he really missed his bathroom from home. He thought to himself that he would never take indoor plumbing and running water for granted again.

Ma set out a plentiful breakfast of eggs and bread slathered with creamy butter. The children drank tea, which was not very pleasant for the Scout twins. They missed their juice and milk from home.

Soon enough it was time to head off to the hedge school.

"Come on now, fill your boots," said Ma as the children laced up their shoes. "Mind your manners and come home straightaway. There are chores to be done." She glanced over at Luke and the twins. "Except for those of you going to Blarney after school," and she gave them a wink.

The boys yanked on their jackets and the girls wrapped their long shawls about them and they headed out into the early morning.

The sun was just slanting across the wet green fields as they stepped out of the cottage. A few chickens and the noisy rooster strutted about the yard and the sheep looked at them expectantly. The Murphys peered down the lane one way, then the other, making sure that there were no soldiers watching them. Then they took off across the fields and towards a barn tucked behind one of the other cottages.

Once inside the barn, the children quickly took their seats at long benches placed against the walls. A few bony looking horses nickered softly at them. A couple of barn cats brushed up against their legs. Izzy reached down and petted one before it wandered off. There were about 25 children there of all ages. The Murphy children introduced Joe and Izzy. A couple of the younger kids giggled when they saw the Scouts. Joe and Izzy started to feel a little out of place. Izzy felt like they were the Murphy family's Show and Tell for the day. "Don't worry," said Siobhan. "You're just different looking and the kids are curious about you. You'll do fine."

After a minute the teacher strode into the barn, closing and locking the door behind him. The children all stood and greeted him good morning.

"Good morning, children. And welcome to Isabel and Joe Scout. I have heard about you. Now all be seated and take out your books. We will begin today with our Latin verbs."

The children were clustered by age. Joe and Izzy were with the older children. They were completely blown away by the other preteens and teens as the Irish kids began practicing their Latin vocabulary. In turn, the Irish kids didn't understand how the Scouts couldn't even speak a single Latin word. "What do they teach you in YOUR school?" one of them asked.

Izzy answered, "We have math, language arts, technology, history, geography and science."

"Well, I guess it's pretty much the same," the Irish kid said, "Except where you have this technology subject, whatever that is, we learn Latin and Greek."

By the end of the morning, Joe and Izzy were pretty impressed with the hedge school. There was a no-nonsense approach to the classes and the teacher made sure that everyone was learning something every moment of the morning. Michael Murphy explained that school couldn't afford to waste any time with the children's learning because everyone had chores to do in the afternoon to help their families survive.

When the teacher dismissed them, Joe and Izzy ran out to the hilltop where Luke was on lookout duty. "How did you like school?" he asked.

Joe laughed. "I loved it! How can you not love a school where it only lasts a half day every day!"

"But I had a little trouble learning all those Latin words," said Izzy. "We've never taken that language in our school."

"Well, we'll fix that right up," said Luke. "We're off on our adventure to Blarney Castle. When you kiss the Blarney stone you receive the gift of gab. Maybe you'll be able to gab better in Latin after you kiss it."

Luke picked up his sack and led the Scouts down a path out of the village into the countryside. "It's about a two hour hike from here so we have to keep a brisk pace," he said. He pulled a loaf of bread and some cheese from his sack. He broke off some pieces for the twins and together they ate and hiked through the beautiful Irish countryside. Luke stopped at a small river, cupped his hands and drank the clear cool water that flowed down from the nearby hills.

Izzy wrinkled her nose. "Luke, aren't you scared that the water is polluted?"

He looked up at her. "Polluted? What's that?"

She said, "You know, when chemicals and garbage are in the water and drinking it makes you sick."

Luke shook his head. "That's crazy! Who puts garbage in water?" And he took a good long drink. Izzy and Joe shrugged their shoulders and drank some of the water too. It was better than

any bottled water they'd ever had. They plopped
down at the side of the river to rest. Trees arched
over the water and little wavelets splashed over
some rocks on the riverbank.

CHAPTER 9

While Izzy and Luke were sipping water and munching on bread and cheese, Joe wandered off along the stream a little way to find some good skipping stones. As he picked his way around a bend he heard some men laughing and talking. He stopped short and flattened himself against a tree along the bank of the stream. He peeked around the side of the tree to see who the men were.

What a good decision to hide! Joe saw three men only ten feet away from him. They too were drinking from the stream and filling up their canteens with the water. They were British soldiers! He knew they were soldiers because they were wearing the famous red coats that he knew the British wore during the American Revolutionary War. They had white shirts and white pants and they were wading in the water up to their knees, which were protected by black boots. Their long hair was snatched back in a ponytail. They were laughing and smacking each other on the back.

"Well now, Newt," called out one of the soldiers, "Are you looking for some newts there in the water?"

The soldier called Newt, responded, "Don't call me that. It's Newton."

"Aw, don't be so priggish," the first soldier said. "You've completely lost your sense of humor since you came back from that war in the American colonies."

The soldier called Newton angrily slapped the water with his fists sending a huge spray onto the first soldier. "That war was a joke. I still don't know how we lost it. We were more disciplined, more intelligent, better equipped and more righteous than those scruffy rebels. If only King George had given us the troops we needed we would have squashed those cockroaches. What a farce! A bunch of untidy hayseed farmers shouldn't have beaten us."

"Is it true that you were there at Yorktown when Cornwallis surrendered?" asked the third soldier.

"I was there," nodded Newton. "A more humiliating moment in my life has never occurred. I had just been released from hospital. My face was still red and raw from the wound that the idiot American colonist had inflicted on me. And to think he used my own bayonet to cut me."

Newton's lip curled and he lifted his scarred face upward. "I swear to you, I will avenge that American disaster. I will restore honor to Great Britain if it's the last thing I do. I will certainly tame these arrogant Irish while I'm on assignment here."

"I don't know," said one of his colleagues. "I don't really think the Irish are all that threatening. I think we're just here to make it look like we're keeping order. The Irish are savages. Look at the way they live – there's no culture, no order, no productivity. I mean, really look at how they live. They have dirt floors, dirty clothing, no schooling. They live with their animals. It's disgusting. It kind of makes you wonder why the King thinks that they're such a threat to us."

"Yea, well, I guess they hate us so much that they'd throw their loyalty to any country that wants to fight us," said the other soldier. "Maybe the King wants to make sure that they don't rebel again, like they did before. That's why we've got to keep them down."

"I suppose you're right," said Newton. "And controlling this Irish colony makes us richer. After all, my own father took over some of their land. He collects the meager rent that the Irish peasants can muster up from their farming and sheepherding. It's not much, but it takes the fight out of the savages all the same."

"Blast it, I've got to succeed here in this assignment, mates," continued Newton. "That fiasco in America humiliated my family. I've got to prove myself to my family and my King. I really want to hurt these Irish. I want to root out all the rebels and string them up as an example. Are you with me?"

"Of course we are!" the other two cried. "Come on, let's rustle up some Irish cockroaches now!"

The three soldiers sloshed back out of the stream and unhitched their horses from their tethers. They swung their legs over their saddles and slapped the reins against the horses' necks. Joe heard the horses wheel around and trot back to the road.   They galloped away throwing up clods of dirt and dust in their wake.

Joe closed his eyes. His knees suddenly felt weak. He slid down the tree trunk until he was sitting on the ground. The Murphys were right. There was real danger here. Those soldiers had so much hatred for the Irish. How could they possibly believe that the Irish were uncultured and uneducated? He'd seen for himself how the village kids all went to school and how Irish culture was so admired, even at great risk to the villagers. He thought how brave the Irish people must be to carry on secretly despite the danger.

He shook his head to try to clear it, and then realized that he'd better get back to Luke and Izzy and warn them about what he had heard. He pulled himself up and ran back to their picnic site. When he got back, he was horrified   He couldn't believe what he saw there. All the blood drained from his face.

Luke and Izzy were lying face up on the ground. Neither of them was moving. Only some flies were buzzing around the remains of their lunch. "NO!" Joe cried. Had the soldiers found them and killed them because they were Irish? But they were just kids. "NO! NO!" he cried again. "I shouldn't have left you. I'm so sorry. NO!" He slumped down to the ground in misery.

Then Izzy raised herself up on one elbow and looked at Joe. "NO, what?" she asked. "What's wrong with you?"

Luke jumped up and faced Joe. "Yeah, what's the matter, Joe?"

Relief flooded Joe. "Oh, thank goodness, you're not dead! I was so scared that the soldiers had killed you." He gestured to where they had been sprawled out. "You were just lying there on the ground."

"We were imagining different shapes in the clouds, Joe," said Izzy. "We weren't dead. Why are you so bent out of shape?"

Joe felt the adrenalin evaporate out of his body. His heart started to beat a little more normally. He pulled his hands through his hair. Then he told Luke and Izzy about the soldiers and what he had heard them say. Izzy clutched his hand. "Where are they now?" she asked him.

"They took off down the road. They were on a mission to find some rebels and kill them," he said. "Maybe we should turn around and go home?" he asked Luke.

Luke shook his head. "No, I don't think we need to do that. They'll be long gone. But you were smart to stay hidden, Joe. This kind of thing happens a lot. We just have to be a little careful. Come on, let's pack up and get to Blarney."

The three of them headed back to the road toward Blarney.

CHAPTER 10

They passed many farmlands and saw the men and women working the fields. Elsewhere pastures were filled with plump sheep and dairy cows. Seeing the gentle cows grazing in the field, Joe broke the silence and said, "Knock! Knock!"

Luke looked questioningly at Joe. Izzy replied with, "Who's there?"

Joe said, "Cows go."

"Cows go who?" said Izzy.

"Cows go 'Moo', not 'who'!" smiled Joe.

"Hey, that's pretty good," said Luke. Do you know any more?"

"Does he know any more!" laughed Izzy. "Joe, here, is the king of Knock Knock jokes."

Joe thought a minute. "OK, here's one more. Knock! Knock!"

Luke caught on. "Who's there?"

"A cow with no lips."

Luke asked, "A cow with no lips who?"

Joe replied, "A cow with no lips says 'ooo', 'ooo'."

Luke laughed. "Ok, let me try one." He thought a minute. "Knock! Knock!"

Joe said, "Who's there?"

"Dragon."

"Dragon who?"

Luke said, "Dragon your feet again!" And he took off running!

The twins grinned and raced to catch up with him.

They continued this way on their journey to Blarney castle. Before they knew it they rounded a bend and saw the magnificent castle off in the distance.

"Oh my gosh!" breathed Izzy as they approached the castle. "It's like a fairy tale. It's a real for goodness castle. Look at those towers and the flag flying from the top. It's beautiful! Do kings and queens live there?"

Luke said, "Well, they used to live there. Now it's a little crumbly and run down. Someone does live there though so we'll have to sneak around a bit to get to the stone."

"What's so special about this stone anyway," asked Joe.

"There are a lot of stories about it. Some say that the stone was the very rock that Moses struck with his staff to produce water for the Israelites when they were escaping from Egypt. Somehow it was brought here during the Crusades."

"Another legend says that it was a gift from a Scottish king to our Irish king when the Irish helped him in a battle against the English. I guess we'll never know how it actually came to be in Ireland. However it got here, our king, Cormac McCarthy, thought the stone was so special that he had it set into his castle when he was building it over three hundred years ago."

"Where does the kissing part come in?" asked Izzy.

"Well, there's another set of stories about that," said Luke. "One story goes like this. An old woman was drowning over in that lake," and he pointed to a lovely lake that they were passing on their right. "As she was gasping for breath and going down, the king was passing by in his carriage. He jumped out of his carriage, threw off his robes and dove into the lake to save her. In return, she rewarded him with a spell. She said that if he would kiss a stone on the top of the castle, he would be gifted with the talent that all of his future conversations would be so convincing and sweet-sounding that he would win all the people over to him."

"I love Ireland," said Joe. "There's so much magic and mystery in everything."

"That's not all," said Luke. "When one of the king's descendants was ruling the castle and all the land surrounding it, the Queen of England wanted to force him to surrender the castle to the Queen as proof of his loyalty. Of course he didn't want to do that. But he lied and told the Queen that nothing would please him more than to turn over his castle to her. But he made sure that something always happened at the last moment before the surrender and she never got the castle. His excuses to her were so numerous and so believable that it became a joke around the English court. Finally, when one of McCarthy's excuses was repeated to the Queen, she said, 'Odds bodikins, more Blarney talk!' So most of us around here believe that if you kiss the Blarney Stone, you are given the gift of gab, just like King McCarthy had."

"The gift of gab," said Izzy. "Joe already thinks I talk too much." Joe pointed his finger at her and nodded big time.

"Well, it's more than just talking," said Luke. "It is being able to get your way by using soft clever speech and humorous words and having your opponent believe that he has won, when actually you are the victor."

"Sweet!" said Joe. "Let's do this!" The large stone castle was now right in front of them.

"Follow me," said Luke. He led them to a side of the castle where there was a narrow slit in the walls. Built into the slit was a steep stairway that couldn't be seen from the outside. The stone steps were damp and mossy and the children had to grab onto the rough stone walls of the castle to keep from losing their balance. They climbed about five stories to the very top of the castle. The roof was flanked by an elaborate parapet and they could see the Irish countryside for miles. The breeze swirled around them and the nearby flag flapped just above them.

"I can see why this would be such a great fortress," said Joe. "If you were being attacked you could see the enemy coming from any direction."

"Yes," replied Luke. "Tis true. It was a great fortress for protection.   And the McCarthys were very powerful kings and protectors. But they were very strong Irish patriots too. They encouraged all of our culture and art. This castle used to be full of poets and singers and artists. They started a school here too and scholars would come here from all over Ireland to read their compositions."

"Where is the Blarney Stone?" asked Izzy looking around. She didn't see anything special about any of the building blocks of the castle.

Luke walked over to the edge of the parapet. "Look down," he said, pointing to the side wall of the castle. Izzy slowly shuffled one foot in front of the other approaching the edge of the parapet. She wished there were a guardrail or a fence or something to keep her from hurtling down to the ground.

"You mean that big stone way down there below us? How are we supposed to kiss it? Won't we fall off the edge?"

"You have to be brave and trust us," said Luke. "You're going to be upside down. Here, lie down on your back with your head hanging over the edge of the wall." When Izzy started shaking her head he smiled, "Don't worry, we'll hold you."

Izzy lay down on the cold stone blocks of the parapet. Luke held tightly onto one of her ankles and Joe grabbed the other one. Slowly she scooched out onto the edge so that her head was hanging in open space. "Joe, don't you let go of me," she warned.

"I won't," he assured her. Inwardly he was thinking that he was glad she was going first. He wasn't sure he'd have the nerve just yet.

Luke gave her more directions. "Now arch your back, stretch out your neck and lean down a little bit more. Find the third stone down from the top and give it a big wet kiss!"

Izzy did as she was told. She just wanted to get this over with before she lost her nerve. She was afraid that she might pass out with all the blood in her body rushing to her head. She gave the stone a quick peck and shouted, "OK, I've done it, bring me back up!" Luke and Joe hauled her back up by her ankles. She sat there, thankful that she didn't get dropped and plummet to her sure death. "Well, I hope this works. I hope it was worth it," she said happy to be safe again.

She looked over at Joe. "Your turn."

Well Joe couldn't be shown up by a girl, so he lay down on his back too. Izzy and Luke grabbed his ankles. He stretched out over the parapet and leaned down to kiss the Blarney Stone. He thought, "If these two even sneeze, they'll let go of my legs and I'll fall. I think this is the most dangerous thing I've ever done in my life. Mom would absolutely freak out if she knew this!" He kissed the stone. It felt cold and clammy on his lips. He called out to the others. "Done! Bring me back up!" They pulled him up and the three of them sat there on top of Blarney Castle grinning away.

"Knock! Knock!" said Joe.

"Who's there?" said Luke and Izzy together.

"Goat."

"Goat who?"

"Goat to believe in magic!" said Joe. "Now we have the magical gift of gab! Thanks for taking us here, Luke."

CHAPTER 11

As the three children hiked the two hours back to the cottage, Izzy needed to ask Luke a question. "Luke, do you remember when you and your brothers and sisters jumped on us out in the field yesterday? You all called me a Banshee. I don't know what a Banshee is. Why did you think that I was one?"

Luke's cheeks reddened and he looked embarrassed. "Yeah, sorry about that. But in our defense, you have got to admit it was a wee bit unusual, you dropping in on us like that."

Izzy smiled. "True enough. But when that happened, you called me a Banshee. Why?"

Luke cocked an eyebrow her way. "Well, you certainly did sound like one when you were screeching at us."

"I call her the Screecher Creature," said Joe. "Is that the same thing as a Banshee?"

"I don't know about that," he replied as they walked. "But here, a Banshee isn't someone that you really want to hear. She's a fairy or ghost, of sorts. She can take on many forms. She can be any age. She can look like a frightening crow, a weasel, or an old witchy hag." Luke looked over at Izzy sizing her up. "She can also take on the form of a stunningly beautiful woman with long pale hair."

Izzy blushed. "Stunningly beautiful?"

"Or a frightening old witch!" added Joe.

Luke laughed. "Either way," he said, "She is known for her keening. It's her duty to wail when a loved one dies. It's supposed to keep the evil spirits away. She can sound like a beautiful angel singing, or like two knotty pieces of wood scratching together. You, Izzy, sounded like the latter."

Izzy scowled.

"The Banshee also acts as a sort of guide to escort the deceased person safely to the other side. When you hear the Banshee wail, you know that someone close to you has either died or will die soon."

"Of course, no one wants to be visited by the Banshee. But she does serve a useful purpose. The family can prepare for the funeral and not be quite so shocked when the death occurs."

"Oh," said Izzy, tucking a loose strand of her hair behind her ear.

"And the long hair is an important feature," continued Luke. "If the Banshee appears in the form of a woman, she can often be seen brushing her long hair with a silver comb."

"Sort of like a mermaid?" asked Izzy.

"Yes," said Luke. "But if you ever see a comb laying on the ground in Ireland you must not pick it up. Maybe we're superstitious …."

"Ya think?" asked Joe.

"….but if you do pick it up, the Banshees, who placed it there to lure unsuspecting humans will pluck you away and you'll never be seen again."

"You tell so many fun stories, Luke," said Izzy. "I love it!"

They continued walking and talking back toward their village. In the fields, the farmers were cleaning their tools and drifting back to their homes. The herds of sheep were being collected and brought back to their pens. Good hearty cooking smells were drifting through the lanes.

As the children rounded the corner to the Murphy cottage they heard a clatter of horses' hooves coming up fast from behind them. They turned their heads and saw three uniformed men galloping towards them. All three brandished silver swords as they charged.

"Soldiers!" said Luke, "Quick, duck here out of the way!" and he pulled them off the narrow lane into the hedge. They cowered there wide-eyed. The horsemen glared at them as they galloped past kicking up clods of dirt in their wake. But they did not stop to bother the children.

Once the soldiers were out of sight, Luke and the Scouts crawled out of their hedge and back onto the road. "Those were the soldiers I saw earlier!" cried Joe. "They said they were going to hunt rebels. Why are they here in our village?"

Luke answered, "They must be hunting down someone they think is violating one of the Penal Laws. It happens a lot. As careful and secretive as we are, sometimes we get caught. We certainly don't want to get caught and get thrown in jail. That happened to one of our neighbors." Luke sighed. "It's a hard way of life. We have to look out for one another. Let's go home. We need to warn Da and Ma that the soldiers are in the village."

CHAPTER 12

As soon as the children entered the Murphy cottage they could tell that something exciting was afoot. Ma was smiling and tapping her foot as she prepared dinner. "Well hello there, darlings. We have a houseguest tonight. Guess who."

Little Claire wouldn't even let them guess, she was so excited. "It's The Candle!" she squealed.

Just as she said that, the tallest man the Scouts had ever seen stepped out from behind the door the children had just entered. He was thin but muscular and had an Afro of red curly hair.

"Pleased to meet you," he said to the twins. "I've heard a lot about you."

The twins shook his hand. "Why do they call you The Candle?" asked Izzy, looking up at him.

He laughed and said, "Just look at me – I'm tall, thin, and very white-skinned, with flaming red hair at the top – just like a candle."

Da added, "The Candle's real name is David Gallagher and he is the roaming Dance Master for our corner of Ireland. He travels from village to village teaching Irish dance steps and feats of strength. We are privileged to have him stay here with us until the festival this Sunday. He will be performing in the dance contests then."

"You're an Irish dance teacher?" asked Izzy excitedly. "I know some steps and I compete too!"

"Do you now?" asked The Candle. "After supper you must show some steps to me. Although I must say I've never seen a female compete as a soloist."

As they were eating dinner, Joe asked The Candle about the feats of strength. That sounded pretty interesting to him.

"So you're interested in learning some feats of strength, are you lad?" asked David Gallagher.

"Maybe I could teach you one or two along with the other boys."

"That would be great!" said Joe. "What are they?"

"They are exercises that we use in fighting …. or competing. With all the turmoil here in Ireland, we need to be able to defend ourselves. When I'm not teaching dance steps, I teach the feats. Tomorrow I am teaching one of the best feats at the hedge school for anyone who is interested. I'm teaching stick fighting. Would you like to learn?"

"Sure!" said Joe.

"Then on Sunday, at the festival, I will demonstrate advanced stick fighting. I understand that there is another dance master from the next county who will be there. It's McGillicuddy. He thinks he's better at it than I am. I plan to show him a thing or two!"

Ma said, "No one is better than you, David. We'll be cheering for you." Izzy loved Ma's loyalty.

"Speaking of fighting, Da," began Luke, "we saw three soldiers riding through the village on our way back from Blarney Castle. Do you think they were hunting anyone down?"

Da looked worried and turned to The Candle. "David, does anyone know you're here?"

The Dance Master shook his head. "I don't believe so. I disguised myself coming into the village. I know that they would like to find me and stop me from teaching dancing, stick-fighting and feats, so I have been extra careful in my travels."

Siobhan said, "But Mr. Gallagher, you're so tall. Even if you disguised yourself, they might be suspicious."

"Well, let's be extra sharp on the lookout, especially this Sunday during the open air festival," said Da.

After supper, and under cover of the cool dark evening, the Murphys and the Scout twins gathered with their neighbors in the hedge school barn where they had classes earlier in the day. There was a Friday night party atmosphere that was born from a long week of backbreaking labor.

The women collected on one side of the barn and traded gossip while the men talked politics and told stories. The kids gathered around Luke and the Scouts and asked them about their adventure to Blarney Castle.

Before long someone pulled out a tin whistle and began playing a lively tune. Someone else joined in and the two whistles wove in and out of each other in happy harmonies. One of the men sat down with the musicians and tapped out percussion on a flat shallow drum with a two headed drumstick. The music was so lively that you couldn't help but feel good about life, despite the troublesome times. Men and women formed groups of eight and danced round and around each other on the straw-filled floor. Long hair was flying, skirts were swirling and laughter rang throughout the barn. The children clapped in time to the music as their moms and dads danced around.

Then it was time for the children to learn some of the dance steps. The Dance Master moved over to one of the horse stalls, fiddled around with the hardware that fastened the door to the stall and removed the entire door. He dropped it down on the barn floor. Dust and straw blew up around it. The barn cats scampered away to hide.

"All right children, gather round," he said as he changed his walking shoes into hard soled brogues. These were very sturdy and rough-looking shoes The Candle had brought with him. The shoes had nails hammered into the leather heels and toes to make more noise as he danced. "I've developed a new hard shoe dance for you to learn. It doesn't have a name yet, but I think you'll like it." And with that introduction he stepped on the horse stall door and began a vigorous stomping and kicking dance. He held his posture perfectly erect with his hands straight down at his sides.

Izzy could not believe her eyes. This was the set dance that she was going to perform at her next competition. It was the dance that she had performed so well at her last dance class that Natalie awarded her the crystal brooch. She loved this dance! She began to do the steps at the same time that The Candle was dancing them. She was so caught up in performing the dance behind The Candle that she didn't notice people all around her stepping back to watch. Soon they had formed a circle around her and The Candle. The two of them were dancing the same steps in unison, he in front, and she just behind him. Both of them kicked at the same time, spun around at the same time, danced on their toes at the same time. Then the dance was triumphantly over.

"Ha! David, I thought you said this was a new dance," said Da. "Our new friend, Isabel, here just danced it step for step with you."

Izzy grinned broadly. "And this dance already has a name. It's called 'Sound the Warning.' It's my favorite competition dance!"

The Candle squinted at Izzy and tilted his head. "But that's impossible. No one knows this dance but me. This is the first time that I've danced it in public. How could she possibly know the steps ....., unless..." and all of a sudden he glowered at Izzy.

"Have you been spying on me, you chit of a thing?" He lunged towards her, eyes straining.

"No! No!" shouted Izzy. "I'm not a spy!" Her shaky legs backed up as The Candle sprang toward her.

Just before he reached her, Joe ran between the two of them. "Stop, Mr. Gallagher! I know for a fact that Izzy hasn't been spying on you. She's been practicing this dance for two months now. She learned it from a different dance teacher, not you. You've got to believe me."

The Candle stopped inches away from the twins. "A different dance teacher? But who?" He thought a minute. "Oh ... sure, and I bet I know who. It's that McGillicuddy chap who wants to fight me this Sunday. Well, I'll show him." He turned away from the twins and spoke to the crowd, "You'll be backing me now, and not McGillicuddy, right?"

"Of course we will!" everyone shouted.

With a final suspicious glance Izzy's way, The Candle warned her, "Don't ever dance that again without my permission! And if you do, you'd sure better be sounding a warning!" and he blended back into the crowd.

At that, the musicians took up their instruments again and the party resumed. As the attention turned away from the Scouts, Izzy placed her trembling hand on Joe's arm. "Thanks, Joe. I think you saved me back there."

Joe shrugged. "Aw, that's ok. It didn't seem fair for him to pick on you like that. And I just didn't think he'd understand the time travel thing." Izzy smiled, "No, that's still hard even for me to understand! But all the same, thanks for sticking up for me."

CHAPTER 13

The next morning was Saturday and all the boys of the village, Joe included, drifted in twos and threes to the hedge school to be taught the art of stick fighting, one of the feats of strength. Izzy, Siobhan and Claire were given the job of taking the sheep out to pasture and spending the day with them as they grazed.

A cool wet mist hung in the air and the girls were happy to wrap their warm long shawls over their heads. Izzy noticed that the Murphy girls brought bags of knitting material with them. "If we'll be with the herd all day, you'll want to bring something with you to keep you busy," said Siobhan.

"Will you teach me to knit?" asked Izzy. "Sure" said Claire and she ran back to the house to borrow Ma's extra pair of knitting needles.

They rounded up the sheep and guided them down the lane to the pasture. As they walked, Izzy asked Siobhan, "How do you and your brothers and sister get along so well? It seems like Joe and I are always at each other's throats. How does your family manage it?"

"Well," thought Siobhan. "I suppose we get along because we have to in order to stay alive here. Everyone pulls his weight and has each other's backs. You know you can always depend on your family when times are tough. But if you want them to help you out when you're in trouble, that means you have to be willing to help them out too."

"Oh," said Izzy. Then she remembered how Joe had stood up for her when The Candle accused her of being a spy. "I think I get that."

When they reached the pasture, they approached a small shepherd's hut. The sheep milled about the hut tearing at the green grass and baa-ing occasionally in content. The girls sat inside the hut to stay out of the drizzle. They opened up their knitting bags and brought out the sweaters that the two of them were working on.

"Those are beautiful!" exclaimed Izzy fingering the sweaters. They were creamy colored garments with multiple twisting and turning patterns of bumps, ropes, and diamonds stitched in. "They are works of art!"

Siobhan pointed out some of the stitches she was working into her sweater. "See this one that looks like a basket? Its name is basket weave. Then there's the ladder, the honeycomb, the diamond, the lobster claw." She pointed to different stitches in Claire's sweater. "These ones are called bobble, plait and link. You can make a sweater with any combination of the basic stitches."

"So cool!" said Izzy. "Will you show me how to do it?"

As Siobhan and Claire taught Izzy how to knit a sweater like theirs, they told her stories about knitting. Izzy was learning that the Irish have a story for just about anything they do.

"See how the yarn looks just like the color of the sheep?" Siobhan asked. "The sheep's natural coats protect them from the rainy weather like we're having today," she said, looking out at the herd grazing nearby. "So when their wool is spun into yarn, some of the natural sheep oil is left in the wool. The sweater acts like a protection from the rain. And the different patterns that are knitted in form little air pockets in the garment that help trap the body's warmth from escaping. That makes the sweaters warm and waterproof, just like the sheep."

Izzy sank her fingers into a nearby lamb's thick wooly back. It felt cozy and warm, and just a little bit scratchy. The lamb turned to her and baahed. She petted his head.

"Beautiful and practical," said Izzy.

"Do you want to hear a story that's a little bit gory?" asked Siobhan.

"Of course!" said Izzy. She reminded herself to remember this story so she could tell it to Joe later. She knew Joe just loved gory stories.

"Well, sometimes different families develop new stitches and patterns. The women in the family knit sweaters for everyone in the family that contain the same types of patterns. The sweaters aren't identical, but you can see how all the sweaters in each family are somewhat similar."

"Like how brothers and sisters look kind of alike, but not exactly alike?" asked Izzy.

"Yes, like that," said Siobhan. "Well, these sweaters are worn a lot by fishermen along the coast. As you can imagine, they need to be warm and dry in all kinds of weather and in all kinds of seas. One day -- now this is the gory part – one of the fishermen must have had an accident at sea and drowned. He washed up on shore three weeks later. Nobody knew who he was because he had been in the water so long."

Izzy and Claire both shivered.

Siobhan continued. "But once they took a look at his sweater, they recognized the lobster claw/basket weave/bobble stitching combination that his family used to knit their sweaters. They were able to return the poor man back to his family for a proper burial."

"Wow," said Izzy. "That's so sad, but kind of clever at the same time."

Then she thought of something else. "Did the family hear a Banshee?"

Siobhan laughed. "I'm not sure if they did or not. But I know someone who could apply for the job and do really well at it!" and she pointed her knitting needle at Izzy.

As the girls continued chatting and knitting, a much less calm activity was occurring at the hedge school.

CHAPTER 14

"YAAAA!" shouted the dozen boys standing in two rows behind The Candle. Their faces looked battle fierce as they pumped their fists into the air.

The Candle strutted in front of them. "Good," he said. "You're all warmed up. Now, the last time we met, I showed you how to use your fists to fight. Today we will learn to use the stick. You will begin by assuming the boxing stance we learned last time."

At that, all the boys arranged themselves into a boxing stance. Joe had never boxed before, but he had watched fighters on TV. He pictured what world-famous boxer Muhammad Ali looked like when he fought, and he hunched himself forward, moving his left hand slightly in front of his head and tucking his right hand into his chin. He formed his hands into C-shapes, imagining how they would fit inside heavily padded boxing gloves. He heard some muffled snickers behind him. He slid his eyes to his left and right. The boys on either side of him did not have the same boxing pose as he did.

They, in fact, looked ridiculous, he thought. They were standing with their backs perfectly straight. Their heads were held far away from their fists. They held their arms in front of their bodies, one pushed further than the other, elbows straight down to the floor. Their fists were closed with their knuckles facing their faces. They looked like the Notre Dame leprechaun mascot. They looked exactly like a cartoon.

He held his pose as The Candle strode over and stood in front of him. "Joe, lad," he said. "What are you doing?"

Joe swallowed. "Um, I'm preparing to box, sir."

"Well, if that's how you're going to fight, Joe, you're going to lose. If you stand like that, your opponent is going to move right in and grab you. Then he'll throw you down into the mud. If he doesn't grab you, his fist will punch you right in the head."

Joe replied, "If he moves in to punch me, I'll block his jab with my own fist here."

The Candle smiled, "Joe, if you try to hit him with your fist, all the bones in your hand will be shattered. It will be the last block you ever throw."

"I'll have my boxing gloves to protect my hands, won't I?"

"No, there are no gloves or wraps. You have no time when you are defending yourself to run home and grab something to wrap your fists with. You are fighting with your bare knuckles. So you must protect them. Here, position yourself like this…." and he showed Joe how to stand properly like the other boys. "Now that your head is back farther there's more space between your head and your arms. With bare-knuckled fighting you can halt incoming fists more safely. It is better to block your enemy's punching arm with your wrist or forearm from farther back than to expose your hands closer to his."

The Candle addressed the whole group now. "Now that you have your fighting stance, we will learn how to fight with the stick. You know, lads, that because of the Penal Laws we aren't allowed to own any weapons. And the soldiers and government officials have their swords and muskets. But that doesn't mean that we can't defend ourselves against their aggression if we have to."

He walked over to the bench at the side of the barn and picked up a walking stick. "This simple shillelagh seems innocent enough to the authorities as we walk around the land with it. But we can use it as a defensive weapon if we need to."

Joe looked at the shillelagh. It was about three feet long and it looked just like the branch of a small tree, right down to the knob at the top. Its bark had been removed and it had been smoothed down the sides. There were a few bumps left in place that looked like smaller branches had once grown out from it.

Each of the boys grabbed a shillelagh and held it with both hands.

The Candle instructed them. "The basic stance for stick fighting is your boxer's stance. Hold the stick evenly in both hands and keep the stick level to the ground, a little below your shoulders. Place each of your hands about a third of the way down from each end of the stick. This will allow you to stick punch effectively with either hand whenever you want." He moved up and down the lines of boys making slight corrections to their stances.

"Now that you have the basic stance down, I am going to teach you how to disarm your enemy when your enemy is holding a weapon towards you." There are two parts. First you will learn what I call, *Greetings*. This technique will throw your opponent off balance and will give you the opportunity to set up your next move. Then you will learn the *Windmill* maneuver that will completely disarm your enemy."

For the next hour, the boys practiced the *Greetings* maneuver. Joe learned that it was a move that allowed the fighter to push into his enemy and deliver a powerful blow to the chest. It could certainly hurt the opponent, but more importantly it would completely surprise him and thus catch him off guard. Once the enemy was off balance, it gave the stick fighter time to set up for his next move.

Once the *Greetings* move was perfected, The Candle taught the boys the *Windmill*. This series of moves had the boys scooping their shillelaghs in and around like the arms on a windmill. Joe thought of it more as the motions he made when he was shoveling snow back home in Illinois.

"Now, I want you to form groups of two and practice disarming each other using the *Greetings* and the *Windmill* techniques," said The Candle.

Luke and Joe squared off and practiced disarming each other. At first it was difficult, and the boys felt clumsy, but after a while they coordinated all the movements and found that they could disarm each other with ease. The Candle spent time with each couple correcting and improving their techniques.

"This is fantastic!" said Joe, breathing heavily.

"I know!" said Luke, leaning on his shillelagh. "We always learn something new when The Candle comes to the village."

They spent the rest of the afternoon practicing some more until they had to return home for evening chores.

CHAPTER 15

That evening after supper, the Murphys were telling the Scouts about the open air festival scheduled for the next day. People from surrounding villages would be coming. There would be contests among the women to see whose homemade bread was the tastiest. There would be a competition to see whose sheep were the plumpest. And if the coast was clear, there would be dance and feats competitions.

The Murphy girls were pulling out their Sunday best clothes and curling up their hair in rags in anticipation of the festival. Izzy watched this hair curling process with interest. The girls couldn't use curling irons to curl their hair because the curling iron wasn't invented yet. Instead, they started with clean wet hair. Then they grasped a strand of hair and folded the center of a strip of old bedsheet in the center of the lock of hair. They curled the strand around the rag and then continued rolling upwards.

When they reached the scalp, they tied the loose ends of the rag on top and knotted it. Siobhan helped Claire do her hair. When they were finished they had rags and bumps of rolled hair sticking out all over their heads like wildly sprouting potatoes. Izzy thought it was a very eco-friendly way to curl her hair, but she was really happy that when she wanted curly hair for a dance competition all she had to do was pin a curly wig to her head.

On the other side of the great room, David Gallagher was huddled with Ma and Da over a stained and torn map of the world.

"I just don't see any other way around it," said The Candle. "It's just too dangerous for me to stay in Ireland any longer. I feel like I'm always just one step ahead of the soldiers. I'm always running from village to village …. always looking over my shoulder to see if I'm being chased. I'm always afraid that my next stop will be a stinking rat hole of a prison. That's no way to live, man."

Da said, "I understand, David. I've always thought that you were pushing the limits of bravery or foolishness -- I'm not sure which, by staying in Ireland. We'll always be grateful for what you've taught us and our children. It's been a privilege to have you stay in our home."

"This situation in Ireland won't last long," continued Da. "I've been hearing from more and more travelers that rebellion is in the air all over this part of the land. Soon we will break free."

"I can't wait for that. I need a fresh start. I think I must leave this week," said The Candle. "After the festival, I'll head to the coast and set sail for America. The colonists there understand religious persecution. More and more Irishmen are going there. There are whole communities of Irish living in America." He pointed to the map. "I've got a cousin who lives in Boston. He can sponsor me."

At the mention of America, Joe and Izzy's ears perked up. They stood up and joined the adults at the table.

"You're going to America?" asked Joe. "How will you get there?"

The Candle said, "There is a ship sailing next week. I've saved up some money and have bought passage. I can start a new life there. I want to marry, settle down, and start a family. I can't do that anymore here where the soldiers are always breathing down my neck."

Joe turned to Izzy with dancing eyes. "Maybe that's how we can get back to America too, Izzy. We can sail back with The Candle."

Izzy shook her head sadly. "No, Joe. I don't think that will work. Even if we could sail back with him, it would still be the 18th century. We wouldn't be able to get back to our family and friends. They live in the 21st century."

"Oh yeah."

"But it was a nice thought," she added. She looked out the window as soft rain fell on the yard, the lane and the village. They had been in Ireland three days now. Even though she had been enjoying Ireland, she was starting to miss her family and her friends. They must be worried sick about her and Joe. Her parents must be frantic. They probably contacted the school and then the police. They probably hung Missing Children posters all around town. Maybe the TV news was broadcasting their pictures all around the country. Amber alerts must be popping up on social media. Her friends were probably crying. And, Ughh! she had missed her dance competition.

But she couldn't think of any way to get back. They could get back to America by taking the ocean trip with The Candle, but what good would that do them? They wouldn't be able to get back to their parents and friends in the 21st century.

It seemed like a hopeless situation. She had trouble falling asleep that night as she tried to find a solution to get back home. She listened to the rain spattering on the thatched roof of the cottage and missed Burr Oaks Glen. "Game over," she thought. "But here are some lovely parting gifts."

CHAPTER 16

Sunday morning's rooster woke the Murphy household up to a world washed clean. Outside the rainwater dripped from the soggy thatched roof. The sun sparkled on droplets clinging to the stone walls. Everyone dressed in Sunday best. The girls unrolled their hair and brushed their gleaming curls. Ma was taking the last loaves of her soda bread out of the fireplace rack and wrapping them in cloth to take to the fair.

"Don't we have to go to church this morning?" asked Joe.

Michael replied, "We do go to church when it is safe for a priest to come to the village. Even then we have to travel to a secret location for church. But this week the roads have been very dangerous for the priests. You've seen the soldiers swarming all over. No one has been able to risk it."

Joe didn't mind missing church but not for this reason. He never thought anyone would have to be so secretive about something that is so normal and safe in America. He would never understand these crazy Penal Laws.

He headed out the cottage door with the others and saw Da reach under the thatch of the roof around the back of the cottage. Da was pulling out a couple of shillelaghs that had been hidden up there. "It's for the competition," he said. He gave them to The Candle who was carrying a bundle of competition clothing. The Candle concealed the shillelaghs in his bundle.

"Well, off we go," said Da, and the family ambled down the lane and out of the village. They proceeded about 15 minutes and then turned off the lane into a heavily forested area.

"Where are we going?" asked Joe.

"There's a meadow in the middle of these woods where we meet for the festival," said Michael. "It's pretty secluded so we shouldn't be disturbed."

They walked single file through the woods, and after about ten minutes they reached the meadow clearing. They saw several other families from the village already there, as well as some people from neighboring villages. A party atmosphere greeted them as they met up with old friends. Ma went over to the soda bread area and arranged her entries for the judging. Some of the men were dragging out wooden planks and nailing them together for the dance competition stage. The musicians were tuning up their instruments.

In addition to the tin whistles and the drums, there were two people who were playing instruments that looked like bagpipes. But the twins noted that they were much softer and less whiney sounding than the bagpipes they were used to hearing.

"They're called the uilleann pipes," said Siobhan. "That's the Irish word for elbow. See, the musician gets air into the instrument by pressing his elbow on the bellows."

"I actually like the way it sounds," said Izzy.

"My favorite instrument is the harp," said Claire. "But no one's going to play it today. It's too far to carry it for the festival."

The twins roamed around the festival soaking in the sights and sounds of an Irish Sunday holiday. Most of the people knew each other and they formed clots of conversation and laughter. There was one gentleman, however, who seemed a bit standoffish. No one was talking with him and he wasn't being very friendly to anyone else. He had a scar running down the left side of his cheek.

Joe watched him out of the corner of his eye. There was something strangely familiar about him but Joe couldn't put his finger on it. The man turned towards him, tipped his head and smiled. Joe waved back at him. As the man lifted his hand to return the wave, the man's cloak parted slightly and Joe saw a glint of steel at the man's side. "That's odd," Joe thought. "I wonder..."

Just as he was forming his thought, the crowd gave a roar and parted in the middle. Striding into the center of the crowd was a powerfully built young man wearing a pleated skirt with the thickest, most muscular calves Joe had ever seen. "McGillicuddy!" shouted some of the people.

"In the very flesh!" replied the young man who would be competing against The Candle. "Now where is that lily-livered David Gallagher?"

"Wow," thought Joe. "He's wearing a skirt and he's trash talking!"

CHAPTER 17

As the crowd egged on McGillicuddy, Joe went in search of The Candle. He found him at the edge of the forest changing into his competition clothing. He had on a skirt too and thick knee socks. He wore a loose shawl-like cape around his chest, clasped at the shoulder to hold it together. He was pulling on his special nail-studded competition shoes. "Hey, Joe laddie, hand me the shillelagh over there will you?" Joe tossed it to him and The Candle twirled it around a bit to warm up his muscles.

"Why are you wearing a skirt?" asked Joe.

"It's a kilt, lad," said The Candle. "It's very traditional. It gives me special powers in a competition."

"Um," said Joe, "this might be too personal, but what exactly are you wearing underneath that kilt?"

The Candle slid his eyes over toward Joe and winked. "My shoes, of course!"

"Oh" said Joe, and smiled at the joke. Then he said, "That McGillicuddy dude is here. He's wearing a kilt too."

"Is he now?" asked The Candle. "Well, let's go say hello to him." He tossed the shillelagh to Joe and the two of them strode off to rejoin the crowd.

The people opened up to let David Gallagher greet McGillicuddy. The two kilted men faced each other puffing out their chests and lifting their chins. "Well, McGillicuddy?" began The Candle. "Well, yourself," he replied poking The Candle in the chest. David Gallagher brushed his hand away and leaned down to the shorter man. "That'll be the last you'll be touching me, man. Let's get on with it."

The two men approached the stage. McGillicuddy pointed over to the musicians and nodded. The musicians struck up a lively tune. Siobhan turned to Izzy. "This is the first competition," she said. "It's a dance off. The audience gets to decide who does the harder steps and who does them better. So you have to cheer really loudly for The Candle so he can win."

"Sounds good to me!" said Izzy. "This is EXACTLY like my dance competitions back home," she thought. "It's the same dancing, but our costumes have a lot more bling on them."

At that both men began to dance to the music at once. Their feet flew faster than a hummingbird's wings as they stomped and tapped on the wooden stage. It was an explosion of sound and fancy footwork. Their legs looked almost double jointed at the knees as they bent them this way and that. All the time, they held their upper bodies perfectly straight with their arms balled into fists at their sides. Then they started leaping and flipping one straight leg in front of the other, clicking their heels together as one leg rose in the air and passed the other leg as it fell.

The crowd clapped in time to the music and the beats the two men were making. Sweat was pouring off the dancers' faces. The onlookers cheered as each man performed a trick better than the other.

After a few minutes, Izzy turned to Siobhan. "How long does this go on?"

Siobhan slowly nodded at the two dancers. "It goes on until one of them drops to the ground in exhaustion."

"Wow!" thought Izzy. Then something caught her eye as she was watching The Candle spin in a circle while on his toes. She bent forward and watched closely. "Oh my gosh!" she said and her hands flew to her mouth. "I've got to find Joe!" Siobhan watched Izzy run off.

"Joe! Joe!" Izzy pulled on his sleeve when she found him on the other side of the makeshift stage. "Look!" she said pointing to The Candle as he danced.

"I know, isn't he awesome?" agreed Joe.

"Yes, but don't you see what he has on?" continued Izzy. Joe shook his head a little, "A kilt?" Izzy grabbed his arm to get his attention. "Look at his cape, Joe. Look what's pinning the top of his cape together!" and she pointed to The Candle's shoulder.

There, glinting in the morning sunshine, unbelievably, was Izzy's brooch. It was the very brooch that she had won at dance class, and that she polished up and brought to school. It was the very brooch that the twins had fought over and was currently sitting on the window sill in Mrs. Sanow's detention room back in Illinois. It was the brooch that had cast a rainbow on the map that brought them to Ireland.

The twins turned to each other in shock. Could it be? Was it the same piece of jewelry here in 1785 in Ireland?

CHAPTER 18

But they didn't have much time to consider this as an angry shout was heard behind them. They turned to see the standoffish man with the scar rushing toward the stage. Joe suddenly realized that it was the soldier called Newton that he had seen by the stream on the way to Blarney Castle. He hadn't recognized him at first without his British uniform. "Gallagher!" the scarred man shouted. "I've got you now, rebel!"

The next moments seemed to pass in slow motion. The scarred man's hand disappeared into his cloak and reappeared with a sharp silver sword. The Candle halted his dance move, looking confused at the interruption. The musicians were still playing and McGillicuddy was still leaping. Then as The Candle saw the scarred man racing to the stage brandishing his weapon, recognition flooded over his face, and he moved to back away from the threatening man. But a nail on his hard shoe caught on the stage and he crumpled to the ground. There was no way he could get away in time. He was sprawled out on the stage and the scarred man was three steps away from plunging his sword into The Candle's chest.

Joe didn't even have a chance to think. Joe was the only person standing between the sword and The Candle. His hand gripped the shillelagh he was still holding and he lunged toward the scarred man. He quickly assumed the Boxer's Stance and performed the *Greetings* maneuver on the soldier. Totally surprised and completely caught off guard, the scarred man hesitated a moment. That was all Joe needed. He flipped the shillelagh into the *Windmill* technique, caught the sword with the end of his stick and flung the sword high over the head of the scarred man. The sword glinted in the sun as it spun end over end above the stage. The soldier's eyes bulged out at Joe as he realized that he had just been disarmed by a mere boy. Joe ran!

In fact, the entire crowd took off running this way and that into the woods once they realized that this soldier spy had infiltrated their festival and very nearly killed The Candle. They didn't want to be caught and hurt as well.

Izzy ran and ran all the way back to the Murphy cottage. She thought her lungs would explode but she kept going. She caught up with the Murphy girls and they burst into the cottage with relief. Luke and Michael were there already looking pretty scared. Pretty soon Patrick and Ma came back too. "This is bad," said Ma. "The soldiers have always been threatening but they've never crossed the line by trying to kill innocent people. This is very bad for the village." Then she looked around the cottage. "Where is Da? And where is Joe?"

After the scuffle at the festival, Joe ran off into the woods. He almost bumped into The Candle and Da. The two of them were talking rapidly. "David," said Da. "They've found you. I don't know how to hide you any longer."

"You've done more than enough for me," replied The Candle. "I cannot put your family in danger. I won't go back to your home. I'll hide out at the hedge school and head for the coast at first light tomorrow. Then it's off to America for me."

He saw Joe and turned to him. "Joe, lad, I've never been prouder of one of my students. You executed the *Windmill* perfectly! You saved my life. Well done, boyo!" And he clasped Joe to him in a great bear hug.

Joe beamed with pride. "You're a wonderful teacher, Mr. Gallagher. The best I've ever had."

Da said, "Let's head back to the village and get tucked away before the spy brings more reinforcements. These are dangerous times, David. We'll walk you back to the village and then split up."

And the three of them headed back cautiously to the village.

CHAPTER 19

Meanwhile, back in the village, all the neighbors were huddled in their cottages. The beauty and joy of the morning had turned into the horror and helplessness of oppression. They worried about the vengeance that the soldiers would carry out on the townsfolk now that they had been deprived of their capture of The Candle. At the Murphy cottage, the family waited anxiously for Da and Joe to return home. "Something must have happened to them," worried Izzy. "Where are they?"

"Be patient," said Ma. "They're smart. They'll wait until it's safe to return home." Nevertheless, she said to Siobhan, "Dear, why don't you go see to the sheep in the front. Let us know if you see anything."

Little Claire clung to Ma's skirts and sucked her thumb. She watched as her older sister bent down to each of the sheep in the front. Even Claire knew that it was a ruse. Ma has sent Siobhan to look innocently after the sheep, but to also watch out for Da and Joe and to report if anything looked wrong down the lane.

The top half of the front door was open and the bottom half was closed to keep the sheep out. Ma leaned on the bottom half of the door and watched casually down the lane. Soon she saw the scarred man. He was riding a grand horse and he had three other soldiers with him. The four soldiers reined up at their neighbor's cottage. They dismounted and entered the cottage. Crashing and thumping could be heard from within. After a while, they left the cottage and went to the next house. They searched that house as well. Then they were outside the Murphy cottage.

Siobhan went pale. They dismounted and brushed past her to the open half door. They spoke brusquely to Ma. "By order of His Majesty, we have the right to search your home for the rebel, David Gallagher." Ma could do nothing, but let them in. They entered the cottage and eyeballed Izzy and the other Murphy children. They went into the back room, turned over the mattress on the bed and poked into the closet.

Back in the main room they overturned the table and chairs just for spite. Then they left as abruptly as they arrived and moved on to the next cottage.

Ma breathed a sigh of relief. She nodded to Siobhan in the front yard. She continued to tend to the sheep, but kept her eyes peeled for any sign of Da and Joe.

Siobhan watched as the soldiers inspected every house on their lane. Then she saw them enter the barn that was their hedge school. She could hear as they were turning over the benches that the children sat on during their lessons. She shuddered realizing that their village's secret had been discovered. She ran up to Ma at the doorway and said, "They've discovered the school. They're staying in the barn. They've ransacked every other cottage in the village. I think they're going to wait for The Candle there."

Ma sighed and lifted her head. Izzy thought that she was saying a silent prayer for the safety of Da. Izzy closed her eyes and prayed that Joe would be safe too.

The minutes ticked by. There was no sound in the village. Time stood still. Izzy could imagine the soldiers waiting in the barn for The Candle to arrive and then to capture him. They would throw him in prison or worse. And for what? He was teaching Irish culture to Irish children. What was the crime in that? It all seemed so senseless to her.

And where was Joe? She was so proud of the way that Joe used the stick to disarm the spy. How had he learned that? She saw Joe in a whole new light. He was a really cool brother, and she was happy that he was her brother. But where was he? And what would the soldiers do to him when they found him? She was so afraid for him.

CHAPTER 20

Suddenly, Siobhan straightened up. She had seen something. She saw Da, The Candle, and Joe cautiously approaching the village.

Then, the three of them were walking toward the path that led to the hedge school, the barn where the four soldiers were waiting in ambush. Siobhan ran to the open door. "Ma, they're headed to the hedge school. I can't shout to them in warning or the soldiers will hear me and catch them."

"What can we do?" thought Izzy. "They can't go to the hedge school. The soldiers are waiting there to ambush The Candle. Da and Joe will get killed too! They don't know that the soldiers are there! I have to warn them!"

Izzy turned to Ma. "Help me get this door off," she said. The top half door was open and swinging on its hinges. Ma and she pried off the hardware that held the door on just as The Candle had removed the stall door in the barn a few days ago. As it swung off the hardware, Izzy caught it and pulled it to the dirt floor of the Murphy cottage. She ran to pull on an extra set of hard shoes where the nails had been hammered into the heels and the toes of the shoes.

Joe, Da and The Candle were on the path to the hedge school. They had no idea that an ambush was waiting for them there.

Izzy stepped on the half door laid on the dirt floor of the Murphy cottage. She started dancing the set dance, "Sound the Warning." How appropriate! She was sounding the warning to Da, Joe and The Candle. She stamped and clicked and made as much noise as possible. Each time her foot landed on the wooden door it sounded like a gunshot. Anyone passing by the cottage would see only the top half of a young girl jumping up and down behind a half door, curls flying and face smiling. They wouldn't see her feet furiously stamping out a warning. The Candle had said, 'I only want to see you do this dance as a warning,' and it was truly a warning this time.

Izzy, Ma and Siobhan watched as Da, The Candle and Joe passed on their way towards the hedge school. Izzy was frantically dancing her set dance to warn them that there was trouble ahead.

Izzy was so frustrated. She could see the three of them furtively making their way toward the hedge school where the ambush waited for them. They thought they would be safe at the hedge school, little knowing that the four soldiers had discovered it and were waiting there for them.

Then, suddenly, The Candle paused. He listened to the pattern of the sounds she was making behind the closed half door. He recognized them. He cocked his head to the side and heard the fury behind her steps. She frantically repeated them over and over.

Then, miracle of miracles, she saw the trio stop. The Candle said something to Da, and he handed something to Joe. Then instead of going to the hedge school, he zigzagged up a hill and ran off in a different direction. At the top of the hill, he turned toward the Murphy cottage. Izzy was still furiously dancing her set dance. She thought that her heart was going to explode. She saw The

Candle. He stopped at the hilltop, turned and he blew her a kiss. Then he was gone.

Da and Joe backtracked toward the Murphy cottage. They entered the yard with the sheep.

Da put his arm around Siobhan and entered the cottage. They were all home again!

Izzy ran up to Joe and threw her arms around him in a big hug. He hugged her back. Then he got embarrassed about the embrace and pulled back.

Da watched and said, "Joe, it's ok to love your family, you know." And he hugged his wife and children.

"When I think of what might have happened," Da said, and he buried his head in Ma's shoulder. "It's ok now," said Ma.

They all sat around the fire. They talked quietly about the soldiers who were waiting in the barn. They would not capture The Candle today or any day. Izzy had warned him off with her loud dance. Da turned to her and said, "Izzy, I want you to know that you warned us about going to the hedge school. As soon as David Gallagher heard you dancing that dance, he knew that something was wrong. He recognized the beats of the dance and knew that only you knew it. He said that you would only perform it if there were trouble. And that warned him to stay away."

Izzy nodded. She knew that The Candle forbade her from dancing that dance because he thought she was a spy. But when she danced it, he knew that she was warning them that there was a trap at the hedge school.

Da continued, "Before he escaped, David Gallagher told me something. He said that first Joe had saved his life with the stick fighting maneuver. And now his sister, Izzy was saving his life by dancing the special dance that only she and he knew. He said that the name of the dance surely was 'Sound the Warning' and he thanked you, Izzy. He was very grateful."

Izzy was flooded with emotions. The dance that the Dance Master had created now had a name. It was 'Sound the Warning.' It all made sense. David Gallagher created the dance, escaped death, sailed to America and taught the dance to Irish students in America. It survived through the years carrying the name, 'Sound the Warning' until Izzy's own teacher, Natalie, taught it to her in the 21st century. The real meaning of the name was actually due to the fact that Izzy herself had sounded the warning to the Dance Master to avoid going to the hedge school to be ambushed. She held her head trying to understand it all. What a magical place this was indeed!

The soldiers in the hedge school must have been very frustrated that evening. They never did catch The Candle. He was long gone to the coast on a sailing ship to America. They would never bother him again. They had no evidence to prove that anyone in the village was doing anything against the laws. They slunk away that night in defeat. Newton would have to live with yet another humiliation.

CHAPTER 21

Back at the Murphy cottage, Ma and Da shook their heads. Things were not going to get any easier for them or for the rest of the village. There would be more rebellion against the oppressors. The village was full of unrest. Things just could not go on as they had. The Irish would have to take back their country.

Joe and Izzy talked quietly between themselves. They were proud of their accomplishments and they loved their foster family in Ireland. But they missed their friends and their family back home. They needed to get back to them.

Joe said, "There's something you need to see." He showed Izzy a bundle that The Candle had thrust into his hands before he escaped across the Irish countryside. The bundle contained his competition costume – his kilt, his hard shoes, and his cape. Attached to the cape was the crystal brooch.

Izzy unpinned the brooch from The Candle's cape. She examined it a bit more closely. Surrounding the crystal were the hammered metal shapes of the heart, the hands and the crown.

Ma saw her looking at the brooch. "You know, that's the claddagh," she said.

Izzy looked up at her. "The claddagh? What's that?" she asked.

"It's a very ancient symbol of Ireland. It's very important to Irish families." She pointed to the clasped hands. "These hands represent friendship, you see. You and Joe are our true friends now. And the heart is a symbol of love."

"And the crown?" asked Izzy.

"The crown is loyalty." Izzy glanced over at Joe. She remembered their Mom always talking about FL – Family Loyalty. She looked down at the ground. Somehow it seemed to make a little more sense now.

Izzy said quietly, "Ma, I think I want to go home now." She looked over at Joe. He nodded at her.

Ma put her arms around Izzy and Joe. "You two came into our lives in a most unusual way. But somehow I think the magic worked. You were meant to be here and we thank you. We love you."

Izzy looked around at the humble cottage. She smiled at the Murphy children who had mugged them thinking they were a leprechaun and a Banshee, but then took them under their wings and showed them how to dance and knit, and how to fight and how to get the gift of gab. They showed them how to be a family. She looked at Ma and Pa who had been so trusting of them and cared for them as they did their own children. She was so fond of them, but she knew it was time to go home.

And she had thought of a way that might just make that work.

CHAPTER 22

"Da, where is that old map of America that The Candle was looking at last night?" she asked. She glanced over at Joe. "Are you ready?" she asked. Joe nodded. He picked up his backpack from school and hung it over his shoulder.

Da uncurled the map on the rough-hewn table in the cottage. Izzy looked it over and saw America. She traced the outlines of Lake Michigan and found the spot where Chicago would be. She then moved her finger slowly toward where she thought Burr Oaks Glen would be – slightly outside of the city limits of Chicago, Illinois.

"I don't know if this will work, but you all say that Ireland is a very magical place. We will always remember you," she said. The Murphys gazed back at the twins fondly.

"We'll miss you," whispered little Claire.

"Aw, Claire, we'll miss you too," said Izzy. "We'll miss you all. And we'll never forget you. Thanks for everything you've done for us!"

Izzy ran and hugged every single Murphy. Then she turned to Joe. "I think we have to hold hands for this to work," she said. "Oh, and you have to tell what point in time we want to travel to."

"Wait!" said Da. He grabbed Joe's arm. "Don't go yet. There's something that I have to know."

"What is it?" asked Joe.

Da turned Joe to face him. "If you and Izzy truly are from the future, then you must know how things here turned out. Tell me truly, does Ireland survive this mess? Will our culture be preserved?" There was such earnest hope in Da's eyes. And he really didn't know what the future held for his family and his country. But Joe and Izzy did!

Joe smiled at him. "You'd better believe Ireland survived," he said. "Ireland is a fantastic freedom-loving country and so many people come to visit it now. And its culture is alive and well, not only in Ireland, but in many other countries where Irish people have moved. You ought to see the St. Patrick's Day celebrations in Chicago. On that day especially, everybody wants to be Irish."

Izzy added, "These days, thousands and thousands of kids learn Irish dancing, and how to play music on traditional Irish instruments. The open air festival we witnessed today is just like some of our Irish dance and music competitions we celebrate in Chicago."

Joe said to Da, "What you, and David Gallagher, and the hedge school teacher are doing now got passed down through the years. It survived."

When the twins finished speaking, Da's sparkling blue eyes brimmed with tears. He said nothing, maybe because he was too choked up. He clapped Joe on the back and nodded his head.

"Thank you," he whispered.

Joe turned to Izzy and nodded. He reached out to hold her hand.

Izzy held The Candle's brooch up to the sunlight streaming in through the half door. The sun caught the prism in the brooch and split it into all the colors of the rainbow beaming down onto the map. Izzy directed the rainbow beam towards Burr Oaks Glen, Illinois, USA. She clasped Joe's hand as he said, "April 22, 2019."

At first nothing happened. A cloud passed in front of the sun in Ireland. Then as the cloud blew off, the rainbow beam pulsed stronger onto the map. Joe and Izzy held hands and felt something tugging them closer and closer to the map on the table. An irresistible force pulled them closer into the map as they followed the rainbow beam. In a blur they watched the Murphy family gaping wide-eyed at them as they directed all their energy into the single spot they thought was Burr Oaks Glen, Illinois. With a swoosh, they were sucked into the map and once again felt the 100 mile per hour wind pulling them further in. Izzy's fingers loosened and she let go of the crystal. It fell with a clatter on the Murphy's table.

They sped along the stream of rainbow colors faster than imagination. The wind tugged at their hair and their skin and their ears were filled with a centuries old rush of time. Joe felt his muscles pull back, helpless as the force ripped them away from 18th century Ireland and back into what they hoped was the present. Izzy held onto Joe's hand and prayed that the time travel would work and they'd be returned to Burr Oaks Glen in the right century. Joe was trying to yell something to her but she couldn't hear him above the noise of the time travel.

CHAPTER 23

Then suddenly the twins were dumped down with a rattle of clanging metal. They were sitting in the pitch dark. Something hard and metallic was at their back. Silence. Then they heard the wet sound of a faucet leaking drop by drop nearby.

"Where are we?" asked Izzy in the dark.

"No clue," said Joe.

"I hope there aren't any spiders here," worried Izzy.

In a moment their eyes adjusted a bit to the dark. They could make out a small line of light near the ground right in front of them. Joe crawled a few feet toward the light. His fingers explored what seemed to be a hard wall above the line of light. His hands moved higher up the wall until he felt something bumping out of the wall. His hand closed upon it. "It's a door knob, Izzy!"

"Be careful, Joe," said Izzy.

Joe slowly turned the door knob and pushed the door open a crack. More light seeped into the small room where they were. Izzy looked around the room. She was sitting next to a metal pail with a mop sticking out of it. There were shelves with cleaning materials lining the walls. "It's a janitor's closet," she whispered to Joe.

Joe peered out the door to see what lay beyond the closet. As his eyes became accustomed to the light outside, he started to chuckle, then to laugh out loud at what he saw.

"What is it?" asked Izzy standing up. "Where are we?"

"Well, my time-travelling sister," answered Joe. "We have landed right in the janitor's closet of our very own school. Right across the hall is the detention room. Our map wasn't very far off at all!"

"Oh Hallelujah!" said Izzy. "We made it back home! Hmm, but what year is it? What day, even?"

Joe opened the door all the way. "Let's explore." He looked back to see if Izzy were following him. "Oh wait a minute, Izzy." He pointed at her Irish shift dress. "You'd better take that off here or there'll be questions for sure. You've got your regular clothes on underneath, don't you?"

Izzy nodded and climbed out of her Irish dress. She crunched it into a ball and tucked it into Joe's backpack. The two of them sidled quietly out of the closet and walked down the hallway. They stopped at the bulletin board. Amazingly the same announcements that were there when they left the school were still hanging. There was a flyer about an upcoming soccer game for the weekend, a school assembly the next week, and joy of joys, the Irish dance competition scheduled for this weekend. They looked at the clock in the hallway.

"Oh my gosh," said Izzy. "It's still recess from the day we time travelled. We spent three days in Ireland and it only took fifteen minutes here."

Joe turned to his sister. "Izzy, we can't say a word of this to anybody. No one would believe it anyway. They'd think we'd gone off the deep end. Let's keep it our secret."

Izzy considered this. Joe was probably right. Everyone would think they were loony tunes if they talked about it. "I guess you're right. I won't say anything if you don't."

Joe nodded. "Well, we'd better get back into detention before they catch us in the hallway and give us double time!"

The twins peeked into the doorway of the detention room. Sure enough, old Mrs. Sanow was still snoring softly at her desk. The old map hung on the wall and the amazing glorious totally magical crystal brooch lay on the window sill. Joe walked over and picked it up. Together they examined it more carefully. It was old and antique looking now, but the last time they saw it, it was fresh and new and it belonged to The Candle. It remained behind them with the Murphy family. It must have been passed down through the family and someone must have taken it with them when he or she was an immigrant in America. That someone must have been a relative of Izzy's dance teacher, Natalie, and she gave it to Izzy. What an amazing journey it had. What an amazing journey the Scouts had.

Just then Mrs. Sanow woke up with a start. Joe pocketed the crystal and the twins quickly took their seats in the classroom. Joe said "Good Afternoon" to Mrs. Sanow. She asked if their essays were finished. "Almost" said the twins at the same time. They tapped out a few sentences on their tablets until the bell rang for afternoon classes.

The rest of the afternoon was a complete blur for Joe and Izzy. They attended their classes as though they were sleepwalking. When the final bell rang, they met up outside the door of the school and walked to the car where Mom was waiting.

As they climbed in, Izzy gave an extra-long hug to Mom. "Gosh, I really missed you, Mom!" she said.

Mom raised one eyebrow at her as she wheeled the car into traffic. "Wow, it must have been some day for you."

Izzy smiled at Joe. "It was truly unbelievable," she said.

Joe reached up to the front seat and handed the brooch to Izzy. "Here, sis. I believe this is yours." Izzy smiled at him. "Thanks, Joe."

She turned to her Mom. "Oh, Mom, this afternoon could you drive me to the yarn store at the mall? I want to get something."

"Well, sure honey," said Mrs. Scout. "But that yarn is for knitting projects. You don't know how to knit."

"Well, someone's been showing me how to do a few patterns," Izzy replied. "I want to knit Joe a sweater."

Mom swung her face towards her daughter in astonishment. "You do?"

"Yep."

Joe said, "And make room for me in the car on Sunday. I want to watch Izzy dance her set dance at the competition." Mom lifted her eyes to the rear view mirror and caught Joe's expression. "You do?" she asked in an even higher voice.

"Yep."

Mom shook her head in amazement. She said under her breath, "Well I don't know who stole my children and replaced them with you two, but I'll take you! What a magical day!" and they drove back home.

ABOUT THE AUTHOR

Christie Sever lives with her husband in a leafy green suburb of Chicago. Her bachelor degree from the University of Notre Dame is in Accounting, and her MBA is from Northwestern University. She worked for many years as a CPA. In addition to raising her own three rascals to become responsible tax-paying adults, she coached hundreds of pre-teens and teens for competition in a Public Speaking club that she founded. She has written many straight news and feature articles for local publications and the Chicago Tribune. Besides kids and writing, she enjoys running her business, Speaker's Edge, a public speaking and presentation skills workshop, and travelling around the world. Meeting foreign children in their homelands through her travels has inspired this book. Whenever she globe-hops, she mentally packs Joe and Isabel with her, as the twins have multiple problems to resolve and many historical times and countries to visit. She anticipates that "Sound the Warning" is the first of a series of books highlighting the culture and history of many different countries in the world.

Please visit our Facebook page:

Children of the World Books

And our website:

https://children-of-the-world-series.business.site

We would love to hear your comments about the books. We also want to hear where you think Joe and Isabel should travel next. Is there a favorite country or historical time period that you think Joe and Isabel would enjoy? Let us know!

We want to hear from you! Your comments and information will always be treated with respect.

Made in the USA
Columbia, SC
29 November 2018